The Fisherman's Fortune

MONUMENTAL BOOKS

The Adventures Of Boubou & Aya : Volume 2
The Fisherman's Fortune
by Walter Simin

Published by Monumental Books

3 rue de Turbigo
75001 Paris
France

www.waltersimin.com

Layout and book distribution by Monumental Books

Printed in 2024

ISBN:
978-2-487769-00-7 (hardcover)
978-2-487769-01-4 (paperback)
978-2-487769-02-1 (ebook)

First Edition

EDUCATIONAL RESOURCES

Dear Parents, Teachers, and Educators,

If you're considering "Boubou & Aya: The Fisherman's Fortune" for educational purposes, or are already using it in your curriculum, we invite you to enhance your experience with our complimentary educational package. Tailored to complement the themes and adventures of the book, this resource is designed to deepen understanding and engagement for young readers.

This dynamic package includes a variety of activities and materials: from reading comprehension quizzes and cultural exploration activities to creative writing prompts and detective skill-building exercises. It's an excellent tool to foster discussion, enhance vocabulary, and encourage a deeper appreciation of the story's themes such as family, courage, and cultural diversity.

We believe that this package will not only support your teaching goals but also enrich the reading experience, making it more interactive and enjoyable. Whether in a classroom, homeschooling environment, or any other educational setting, these resources are here to help you bring the magic of "Boubou & Aya" to life.

www.waltersimin.com/downloads/

Enjoy the journey of learning and adventure!

ACKNOWLEDGEMENTS

To my dear friend Seydina, whose invitation led me on an
unforgettable adventure in Africa, a journey that filled my heart
with stories and my soul with memories. Our shared adventure has
inspired the tales of Boubou and Aya. Your friendship is a treasure
I deeply cherish.

This book is for your brave son, Grillou. May the light of his mom,
now among the stars, always guide his path. To Grillou and all the
children of the world: may you find endless adventures in the pages
of books, where the magic of life resides. Through reading, may you
travel far and wide, finding peace, solace, and the incredible joy of
discovery. Let stories be your compass and your comfort,
as they are mine.

With heartfelt gratitude and love,

Walter Simin

The Fisherman's Fortune

WALTER SIMIN

Contents

CHAPTER ONE

The Fisherman's House

EIGHT SHINY NEW BIKES AND A SLEEK MOTORCYCLE WITH A sidecar cruised along the beach road, heading out of town. The road wound around the bay's edge, which sparkled like a gem in the sun. It was a perfect Saturday morning in June, the kind that makes you feel excited just to be outside. The summer heat was crazy hot, but the ocean breeze felt amazing as they rode along.

This group of middle and high school friends shared a special bond. They went to Zinguichou High School together and were always ready for an adventure, especially on weekends when they could escape the city's heat. These weren't just any old bikes they were riding. They were presents from two of the kids in the group, Boubou, and Aya, who had gotten them as a reward for helping solve the lighthouse mystery. Their grandma had suggested saving the money for important stuff, but in the end, she agreed the bikes were a great way to celebrate their teamwork.

When they got to a spot where the main road met a dirt path, the kid in the lead slowed his bike to a stop. It was Boubou, a tall sixteen-year-old who always seemed to be thinking up new plans. He waited for the rest of the group to catch up.

"So, where to next?" Boubou asked, grinning with excitement at the prospect of discovery.

The others parked their bikes and hopped off, wiping sweat and stretching. Aya, Boubou's thirteen-year-old sister, shook out her curly hair in the wind. Her bright eyes were full of mischief. The rest of the gang included Adama Sambou, the eldest and a close friend of the Diouf siblings; Bouma, whose muscles hinted at his passion for boxing; and their schoolmates Bacary, Djily, Mouhamed, Pierre, and Amath. Each shared a bond, not just of friendship but of countless memories and adventures.

Usually, you could find them on the soccer field after school, playing hard and laughing harder. But today was special. They were taking their first big ride on the new bikes that Boubou and Aya had gotten them after they cracked the case of the missing diamonds at the town's lighthouse. It was a wild story they loved telling again and again, each time with a few extra details thrown in. They still couldn't believe how they had outsmarted the local police and found the loot!

"Remember when you figured out you searched the wrong lighthouse?" Bouma said, his eyes lighting up at the memory.

"And the look on the Chief's face when you handed them the stolen diamonds!" Bacary added, laughing.

"As if the police could ever solve anything without us," Aya said, rolling her eyes. "Remember how they thought the thief's last words meant the town's lighthouse, not the old lighthouse abandoned train station by the cliff?"

"Yeah, and just when you thought you were out of luck, you figured out he was talking about the train station," Bouma added with a chuckle. "You have a real gift, Aya!"

"Detective Diallo and Constable Sarr, the dynamic duo of disappointment," Aya quipped. "If only they were as good at their jobs as they are at playing cards."

As they continued along the beach road, Boubou noticed something unusual. "Hey, look out there!" he exclaimed, pointing towards the bay. The group turned to see two motorboats in the distance, one seemingly chasing the other. The distant roar of their engines faintly reached their ears.

"Looks like some kind of chase," Aya said, shading her eyes with her hand.

"Weird, isn't it?" Djily said. "Maybe it's nothing, but it feels kind of intense."

They all watched for a moment, but the boats soon disappeared from view as the road curved away from the shore.

"Wonder what that's all about," Boubou muttered as they continued their ride.

As they reminisced about their lighthouse adventure, Boubou noticed something unusual. "Hey, did anyone else hear that?" he asked, his face suddenly serious.

The group quieted down, listening intently. "Hear what?" Djily asked, looking around.

"I thought I heard... I don't know, like a distant cry or something," Boubou replied, straining his ears.

Aya smirked. "Maybe it's the wind playing tricks on you, big brother."

Adama, always curious, chimed in. "Or maybe it's another mystery waiting for us. Remember, this area has its share of spooky stories."

"Like what?" Pierre asked, intrigued.

"Like Kambossa's place," Adama said, pointing to a cliff in the distance. "See where the road disappears? Right there. You can't miss it."

"Kambossa's old place?" Boubou echoed, a mix of excitement and apprehension in his voice.

"Yeah, we've never explored there before," Adama said, his eyes lighting up.

Boubou looked a bit worried. "I rode by it once but never went close. It's kind of creepy."

"Who's Kambossa?" Pierre wondered.

"He was the guy who used to live there," Boubou explained. "But he died. He was murdered."

Pierre's eyes went wide. "Murdered? Is that why they say it's haunted?"

"I don't believe in ghosts," Djily said, "but there've been some weird stories about that place ever since he died." Djily, often the skeptic of the group, had a knack for remembering local legends and stories, which he loved to share, especially if it added a chill to their adventures.

"Kambossa was pretty strange," Pierre added. "I mean, what fisherman builds a house way up on a cliff instead of by the water? That's like a baker who doesn't like bread."

Bacary nodded. "Exactly. Most fishermen live right by their boats. Kambossa was different."

Kambossa's house was in an unusual location, perched atop a steep cliff high above the bay, isolated from everything else. The kids had already ridden their bikes about two miles from town, and Kambossa's place was still another three miles ahead. They could only see it because it stood out so much against the sky.

"He was a real loner," Boubou said. "A mystery man. He never wanted anyone around."

"Plus, he had these mean guard dogs," Djily added. "No one wanted to go near them. People stayed away unless they had to."

"And don't forget, he was a total cheapskate," Aya said.

Boubou grinned at his sister. "Well, people said he was rich. At least, that's what everyone thought."

"Yeah, everyone talked about how he had tons of cash stashed away. But when he died, they didn't find a single penny in his house," Bacary said.

"Kambossa always said he didn't trust banks," Adama added. "But who knows where he got all that money. He never seemed to work and hardly ever came to town."

"Too much money always leads to trouble," Amath said seriously. Amath was known among his friends for his cautious nature, often thinking ahead and weighing the risks of their adventures.

"Maybe he inherited it?" Pierre suggested.

"Could be. Kambossa must've had money at some point to build that huge stone house. It's probably worth a fortune," Boubou said.

"Does anyone live there now?" Pierre asked.

Everyone shook their heads. "It's been empty since he was killed," Boubou explained. "I don't think anyone would want to live there."

"It's so far from everything," Aya pointed out. "And all those spooky stories about it sure don't help."

"I don't believe in ghosts," Djily said, "but there is something weird about that place. People have seen strange lights there at night."

"Especially on stormy nights," Adama said, lowering his voice. "One time, a guy's car broke down near there. He didn't know about the spooky stories, so he went to the house for help. Big mistake!"

"What happened?" Pierre asked, leaning in.

"Well, he thought no one lived there when he entered the yard. But just as he was leaving, he saw an old man staring at him from an upstairs window," Djily said, building the suspense. Djily had always been fascinated by the supernatural, even though he claimed not to believe in it. His curiosity often got the better of him, leading him into situations that tested his skepticism.

"He yelled up at the old man, but he just vanished!" Adama added. "The guy searched the whole house but couldn't find anyone."

"That's when he got out of there fast," Mohamed said, making everyone jump. They had nearly forgotten he was there.

Pierre's eyes sparkled with excitement. "I don't blame him for running, but I really want to see this house now. Let's do it!"

"Yeah, let's go!" the others agreed.

Adama laughed. "Okay, follow me! It'll take a pretty brave ghost to scare all of us away."

Their bikes gleamed in the sun as they rode down the beach road towards the mysterious cliff-top house. What had started as a fun ride had turned into a real adventure. All of them, except Pierre, had passed by Kambossa's place before, but they had never dared to leave the main road and explore the secrets of the old abandoned mansion—until now.

❖

The path to Kambossa's house was nearly obscured by overgrown weeds and bushes, making it difficult to see. Even when Kambossa was alive, he didn't take care of it much. The house was hidden by trees, so you couldn't spot it from the main road. Most people avoided the place, whether they believed in ghosts or not. The stories that had been going around about the big stone house since Kambossa was killed two years ago were enough to make anyone think that weird things happened there. But no one knew for sure if it was really haunted or not.

Kambossa's murder had been a big shock to everyone. He was an old fisherman who, as Aya had said, was known for being really cheap. He was also kind of odd, and some people even thought he might be a bit crazy. How he lived alone in that big house only made the whole thing seem more mysterious and scary.

No matter what people thought of him, the whole town was stunned when they found out the old fisherman had been shot dead in his own kitchen. It looked like a robbery gone wrong. Everyone had always said he must have a lot of money hidden away in his house. Still, even after the police searched everywhere, they never found a penny.

"And of course, the police were no help at all," Aya said, shaking her head. "They couldn't find their own badges if they dropped them."

"Yeah, it took them forever just to figure out it was a robbery," Boubou added, rolling his eyes. "And they still couldn't find anything."

"Maybe we should give them a map next time," Aya said with a smirk. "Or better yet, just solve the case for them."

There were all sorts of wild guesses about where he got his money from in the first place. One story was that he had found gold in the ocean, and that's why someone might have killed him—to get their hands on this secret treasure.

This was the creepy history of the place that Boubou, Aya, and their friends were now heading towards, feeling nervous and excited. To make things even spookier, as they got closer to the cliff where the house was, the sun went behind some clouds, making everything look dark and gloomy.

As they approached the house, a low rumble of thunder echoed in the distance. Boubou looked up at the sky, seeing ominous gray clouds rolling in from the east. "Looks like a storm is coming," he said.

The group exchanged uneasy glances. "Do you think we should turn back?" Bacary asked, eyeing the darkening sky.

"Not a chance," Boubou said firmly.

Before long, they arrived at the overgrown driveway leading to the supposedly haunted house. The path was so covered in weeds and plants that it was hard to see, but they still managed to ride their bikes through it. They kept going until they reached a rusty old gate blocking their way. Boubou got off his bike and gave the gate a hard kick. The chains holding it closed broke apart with a spooky clank, and the gate swung open. The group rode on into the yard.

Kambossa's place started to feel even creepier as the sky got darker. The grass was tall and wet, and weeds and prickly plants were growing everywhere, making it hard to see the path. The wind picked up, howling through the trees and making the grass whisper like ghosts. It all made the kids feel like they were riding straight into a scary movie.

Pierre glanced around nervously. "This place is really giving me the creeps," he muttered.

"Wait until you see the house," Djily said, sounding both nervous and excited. Djily had always been fascinated by the supernatural, even though he claimed not to believe in it. His curiosity often got the better of him, leading him into situations that tested his skepticism.

A shiver of fear ran through the group as they finally saw the old stone house. It looked like it was about to be swallowed up by all the trees, bushes, and weeds growing around it. The front door was almost completely hidden behind the weeds, and the bushes grew so high they reached the windows on the first floor. Tree branches hung over the roof, and a single shutter, barely attached by its hinges, suddenly banged loudly in the wind.

Other than that, the house was eerily quiet. With the dark, cloudy sky above, the place seemed to give off a scary feeling of gloom and dread.

Aya, always the brave one, spoke up. "Well, we made it. Let's check it out."

Adama tried to laugh it off. "No ghosts yet!" But even though he was the biggest of the group, you could tell he was a little freaked out too.

Djily, who had been quiet, shook his head. "I don't know about this, guys. This place gives me the shivers."

"Don't be such a chicken," Aya teased. "It's just an old house."

"An old house where someone was murdered," Amath added, his eyes wide. "Do you really think it's a good idea to go in there?"

Boubou took a deep breath, trying to steady his nerves. "Come on. If we stick together, we'll be fine."

Aya nodded in agreement. "Exactly. We can't let fear stop us. We've faced worse before."

"Easy for you to say," Djily muttered. "Boubou said he heard noises."

"What noises?" Bacary asked, raising an eyebrow.

Boubou hesitated. "It sounded like... a cry or something. Coming from the direction of this house."

Amath shivered. "Great. Just what we need—crying ghosts."

Boubou put on a brave face to reassure the group. "Look, we can handle this. We've solved tougher mysteries. Let's just take it one step at a time."

Aya smiled encouragingly. "That's the spirit. Come on, let's go."

They left their bikes under a tree and walked up to the run-down house. As they cautiously approached it, the wind picked up, rustling the leaves and making the old shutter bang even louder. The group huddled closer together, their earlier bravado fading as the eerie atmosphere surrounded them.

Boubou led the way, pushing through the overgrown bushes to reach the front door. He glanced back at his friends, offering a reassuring smile. "Ready?"

"Ready as we'll ever be," Aya said, her voice barely above a whisper.

The front door was barely attached to its hinges and creaked open when Aya pushed it.

"I can't believe someone used to live here alone," Adama muttered, glancing around nervously.

"I know, right?" Aya replied, her eyes wide with wonder. "This place is huge and so creepy."

"Imagine living here on your own," Pierre added, shivering a little. "All these dark, empty rooms... It must have been so lonely."

"And scary," Boubou chimed in. "Especially at night. Every little noise would probably freak you out."

"It must have been less creepy when it was nicely decorated," Aya suggested. "I bet Kambossa had it looking pretty fancy back in the day."

As they stepped into the hallway, it was so dark they could hardly see. The windows in the back were boarded up, so only a few thin beams of light came through, showing all the dust that covered everything. There was a staircase in front of them going up and a closed door on the left.

"This must be the living room," Aya said as she boldly pushed the door open.

The room was empty except for a stone fireplace on one wall. As the group walked in, a rat suddenly ran out from the fireplace and across the floor, disappearing into a hole in the wall. Everyone jumped, already feeling spooked out by the creepy house.

"It's okay, just a rat," Boubou said calmly, helping everyone relax.

"Well, that was a nice welcome," Pierre joked, trying to lighten the mood. "Seriously though, how did Kambossa manage living here alone?"

"He must have been really brave or really crazy," Adama said, shaking his head. "Or maybe a bit of both."

They all gathered in the empty room, unsure what to do next. Aya, curious, went over to the window and looked out. But the view of tangled trees and weeds under the darkening sky only made things feel even gloomier. She quickly came back to the others.

"What now?" Adama asked, breaking the silence.

"There's not much here," Aya said, slightly relieved. "It's just a dirty old house. Maybe we should go upstairs and—"

She was suddenly cut off by a scary sound.

From somewhere upstairs, a bone-chilling, shaky scream rang out, sounding like someone absolutely terrified. The sudden, spooky noise made everyone freeze in fear, their eyes wide.

The haunting cry echoed through the quiet, dusty halls of the old Kambossa house, making their adventure feel much more frightening than fun.

CHAPTER TWO

Shadows And Thunder

THE SCREAM THAT PIERCED THE AIR WAS UNLIKE ANYTHING the kids had ever heard. It was creepy and blood-curdling, almost like a monster's howl, but definitely human. As the terrifying sound faded away, the old, falling-apart house seemed to mock them, bouncing the echoes around until they disappeared.

The kids stared at each other, their eyes wide with fear. For a moment, nobody said a word. Then Djily's shaky voice broke the silence. "No way I'm staying here!" He ran for the door, tripping over a loose floorboard and nearly falling flat on his face.

"Wait for me!" Pierre yelled, running after him, but as he bolted, he accidentally knocked over an old vase that shattered loudly, making everyone jump. Adama Sambou was right behind them, not wanting to be left alone.

Aya stood her ground. "Hold on," she said firmly. "Don't you want to know what's going on?"

Boubou looked torn between running away and staying with his brave sister. He looked scared but didn't budge. "Aya, are you sure?" he whispered.

"You're on your own," Amath said, his voice shaking. "This place is haunted! I'm not hanging around to find out why." He bolted out into the hall, but not before getting his shirt caught on a doorknob and struggling to free himself in a panic.

"There's probably a normal reason for all this, but I'd rather think about it from somewhere safe," Amath added, finally freeing himself and hurrying after them. Known for his pragmatic approach, Amath was always the first to suggest retreat when things got too risky.

Bouma, careful but quick, added, "You can't fight what you can't see," and swiftly left, but not before stumbling over his own feet and nearly crashing into the wall.

Mouhamed paused, glancing back at Boubou and Aya. "I guess I'll—," he started, but then stumbled and bumped into the wall. "Oops! Sorry!" he blurted out before dashing outside, nearly losing his shoe in the process.

The boys had escaped the spooky house, their footsteps fading into the night. Boubou and Aya listened as their friends ran away. Boubou shrugged and turned to his sister. "Looks like we lost everyone," he said. "Should we go too?"

Aya sighed and looked around. "Yeah, let's get out of here," she agreed, sighing in relief. They walked into the hallway, Aya glancing up the dark staircase. But it was too dark to see anything. The upstairs was hidden in shadows, and the silence was even creepier than before.

❖

When they got outside, they found their friends huddled under the trees, far enough from the house to feel safe. The group was excitedly talking about the scary noise. As Boubou and Aya walked up, they heard Pierre say, "I don't need any more proof. That house is definitely haunted."

"It was just a noise. No need to run away," Boubou said, trying to make everyone feel better.

Aya, always brave, added, "It would've been different if we actually saw something. I don't believe in ghosts. Why don't we go back and check it out? Running away is silly."

Adama and Djily, feeling a bit embarrassed about running out while the Dioufs stayed calm, looked at each other. "That sound scared me more than anything," Adama admitted. "But I'll go back if that's what we decide."

Aya turned to Bouma. "What do you think, Bouma? Ready to face the mystery?"

Bouma thought for a moment, scratching his head. "Well, I'm not exactly excited to go back in," he confessed. "Not that I'm scared or anything!" he added, a little too quickly to be believable.

Aya smirked. "Aya smirked. "Right, and I'm the tooth fairy."

Amath jumped in, waving his hands. "But what if there's, like, a ghost dog or something? I'm allergic to dogs!"

Aya raised an eyebrow. "A ghost dog, Amath? Really? I didn't know ghost fur caused allergies."

"But really, what are we going to find in there?" Amath asked, still unconvinced.

Boubou looked at the group, noticing how they avoided eye contact. He announced, "Aya and I are going back, no question. We have a mystery to solve."

Bacary suddenly had an idea. "We need backup!"

Aya laughed a little. "Backup? There are already nine of us, more than the whole police department."

Realizing how silly his suggestion was, Bacary's face brightened. "Right, you two are great at mysteries! This could be the perfect chance for some detective work."

He was talking about how Boubou and Aya were known for their detective skills, something they got from their dad, Malik Diouf. Malik had been a famous detective, first working for the Zakar police and then starting his own successful detective agency in Zinguichou. He was known as an amazing investigator all over Africa. Sadly, Malik and his wife died in a strange car accident, leaving Boubou and Aya determined to continue their dad's legacy.

Their mom had wanted them to become doctors or lawyers, but the excitement of detective work, which their dad had been so good at, was too hard to resist. Even after their parents died, Boubou and Aya were set on proving how good they were and becoming top detectives themselves.

The Diouf siblings had become famous for solving mysteries when they cracked the diamond and jewel robbery case at the famous lighthouse in Zinguichou. Their success was all anyone talked about in town, and the surrounding areas, and the story grew with each retelling. They had outsmarted everyone—the local police, the confused Countess, and even the Countess' brother.

"So, what's the plan, Boubou?" Adama asked, breaking the brief silence that had settled over the group.

"We need a strategy," Boubou replied. "First, we should split into smaller groups to cover more ground. We have to figure out where that scream came from."

Aya nodded in agreement. "And stay in touch. If anyone finds anything, shout out to the rest of us. We need to stay connected."

Djily hesitated, glancing back at the house. "Are we sure about this? I mean, what if there's something really dangerous in there?"

Aya rolled her eyes. "Djily, the most dangerous thing we've seen so far is a rat. Unless you're afraid of tiny teeth?"

"We won't know unless we check it out," Boubou said firmly. "We've faced tough situations before. We can handle this."

The group exchanged determined glances, their initial fear slowly turning into a resolve to uncover the mystery.

"Okay, let's do this," Bouma said, trying to sound more confident than he felt. "But if we see any ghost cats, I'm out!"

Aya chuckled. "Oh, it's ghost cats now? Seriously, Bouma?"

"Or dogs, whatever," replied Bouma, sheepish.

As they prepared to head back, a sudden loud noise echoed from the house, making everyone jump.

"What was that?" Pierre asked, his voice trembling slightly.

Aya took a deep breath. "Just the wind, probably. Let's stick to the plan. We'll be in and out before we know it."

Djily was torn between not wanting to go back and not wanting to seem like a coward. "Uh, my mom said I need to be home before dark," he mumbled, even though it was still afternoon.

Aya gave him a knowing look. "Sure, Djily. And I must feed Amath's ghost dogs their ghost dog food." Then she turned to Adama: "What about you, Adama? Did you leave the stove on or something?" she added sarcastically.

Boubou rolled his eyes. "Come on, guys. We can do this."

Just then, dark storm clouds, which had been gathering for the last hour, suddenly let loose. A strong wind shook the trees, making the bushes shiver, and then heavy raindrops started falling. Within moments, it was pouring rain.

"The bikes!" Boubou shouted, getting everyone's attention.

They quickly ran through the wet grass to where their bikes were parked, pulling their coat collars up against the rain.

Boubou, always quick to find a solution, yelled over the rain, "There's an old shed nearby! We can keep the bikes dry there."

They found the old wagon shed near the back of the house. It was falling apart, but the roof was still mostly in one piece. They quickly wheeled their precious bikes under it, happy to be out of the rain.

With the bikes safe, Aya's adventurous spirit came back. "Okay, let's go back to the house," she urged, sounding determined.

She took off from the shed, running through the pouring rain with Boubou right behind her. After a moment of hesitation, the others followed, pulled in by the mystery and the Diouf siblings' brave spirit.

The storm still raged around them, adding to the eerie atmosphere. Lightning flashed, illuminating the old mansion and casting long, spooky shadows.

The group huddled together in the old kitchen, now a temporary shelter from the storm, their clothes soaked and hearts racing. The heavy rain pounded against the broken windows, and the roof drummed with the downpour. Thunder rumbled in the air, and lightning flashed through the darkness, lighting up their worried faces.

Trying to make the best of it, Adama wrung out his soaked cap while the rest looked at the wild storm. The second scream cut through the storm's noise like a knife in this tense quiet. It was a chilling echo of the first, a haunting wail that seemed to reach into their very souls. The scream faded, only to be replaced by a loud thunderclap that felt like the sky was splitting apart, making the rain pour down even harder.

In the shadowy, dusty kitchen, the group looked at each other with wide eyes, a mix of fear and determination. Boubou broke the tense silence, his voice firm. "I'm going to find out what's behind this," he declared, moving towards the door that led inside the house.

"I'm with you," Aya said, her voice steady.

Encouraged by the Dioufs' bravery, or maybe too scared to stay alone, the others quickly lined up behind them.

Boubou pushed open the door, stepping into the next room. It was dimly lit, with a bit of light struggling through a boarded-up window. As their eyes adjusted, they could see another door across the room, leading to a different hallway on the side of the house, not the one they had seen before. Feeling nervous and curious, the group moved forward, approaching the unknown ahead.

A sudden, deafening crash sent a sharp shiver down their spines. The boys, frozen for a moment, looked at each other with fear and determination.

Boubou, always the leader, kept his voice steady. "We need to find those stairs," he insisted, his mind set on figuring out where the eerie sounds were coming from. "That scream definitely came from upstairs."

With careful steps, they made their way through the room, the storm outside providing a dramatic background. Lightning flashed through the cracks of the boarded window, casting ghostly shadows across their path.

As they moved, a strong gust of wind shook the house, slamming the door shut with a startling bang. The sudden noise made everyone jump in surprise.

Djily, closest to the door, frantically twisted the knob, pulling and pushing, trying desperately to open it again. "It's locked," he gasped, the dread evident in his voice.

Amath's fear grew. "This is it; we're doomed," he declared, his voice full of panic.

Bouma, trying to be the voice of reason, threw his weight against the door, but it didn't budge. "I can't believe how solid this is," he grumbled, rubbing his shoulder.

"If we even make it till tonight," Amath exclaimed, his anxiety rising.

Boubou, trying to stay calm, reassured them. "We'll find another way out. Let's check the side hallway."

As they moved across the room towards the hallway, an even more chilling howl echoed through the house, amplified by the empty space. It was met with a flash of lightning, revealing their startled faces.

With a burst of adrenaline, they charged into the narrow, dust-filled hallway. Their footsteps thundered against the old floorboards.

Then, another loud crash sounded, seeming dangerously close. The boys stopped in their tracks, hearts pounding, as they faced the unknown dangers of the mysterious old house.

Amidst the chaotic whirl of dust and debris, the boys were in a dire situation. Plaster and lath rained down on them, a deluge of ruin from the crumbling ceiling. They were knocked to the ground, surrounded by a choking cloud of dust that filled the air, making it hard to see and breathe.

"Run for your lives!" yelled Boubou.

His warning cry had barely faded when the structure above groaned ominously, signaling further collapse. Now struggling with fear and confusion, the boys scrambled desperately to find shelter or a way out. The house, it seemed, was falling apart around them, unable to withstand its age and the fury of the storm.

The crackling and splintering above got louder, a terrifying soundtrack to their situation. Then, with a deafening roar that was even louder than the first, another section of the ceiling gave way, unleashing a second wave of debris. The force of it bore down on them with relentless ferocity, pinning them under the weight of broken wood and plaster.

Amidst the chaos, the question hung in the air, unspoken but clear in the minds of each of the boys: Was the Kambossa house really collapsing around them? The thought fueled their panic as they struggled against the overwhelming mass of wreckage, desperately seeking a way to escape the crumbling walls of the old house.

CHAPTER THREE

Out Of Gas, Out Of Luck

THE STORM CONTINUED TO RAGE, BUT IT WAS MERELY background noise compared to the creaking and cracking of the collapsing house. In the middle of the chaos, Boubou's instincts kicked in, allowing him to shield himself as best as he could from the shower of debris. Thankfully, the materials weren't too heavy. As the cascade of plaster and wooden laths slowed down, he realized he wasn't hurt, just buried under a pile of rubble and choking in the thick cloud of dust.

His first thought was for Aya. Scrambling to his feet, pushing through the debris, his eyes searched frantically for his sister. A glimmer of hope sparked as he spotted a slender arm reaching out from the wreckage. He quickly grabbed the hand, pulling his sister to safety. To his huge relief, Aya was shaken but not hurt.

The others, too, were gradually freeing themselves from the debris. In a matter of minutes, all nine friends, covered in dust and looking messy, had gathered in the clearer space in the hallway. Djily and Amath complained of bruises but, thankfully, weren't seriously hurt. Amath made quite a fuss about his discomfort in his typical dramatic way.

Looking like a giant ghostly figure covered in dust, Adama was the first to say what they were all thinking. "We need to get out of here," he gasped, his voice filled with urgency. He looked around, desperate for an exit.

Just as eager to leave, Boubou noticed a door on the side of the hallway. "There's a door there," he pointed out with relief.

Bouma, taking charge, moved to the door and tried to open it. He pushed and kicked with all his might, but the door stayed firmly shut, stubbornly refusing to budge. The realization that they were locked in added a new layer of urgency to their situation. The group exchanged worried glances, the need to escape the crumbling house now more pressing than ever.

"A window, guys!" Aya exclaimed with a spark of hope. "We can break out through here."

The window, though boarded up, already had its glass shattered. Adama and Boubou grabbed stones from the fallen walls and ceiling debris and began hammering at the wooden planks.

"We need to keep moving," Amath suggested urgently. "Who knows if the rest of this place will collapse around us. We might not be so lucky next time."

With a crack, one of the window boards gave way, revealing the rain-soaked world outside—trees and bushes drenched in the downpour. Another round of pounding with the rocks, and yet another board fell, leaving a gap just big enough for them to squeeze through.

"Wow, that's our ticket out of here!" Boubou couldn't help but smile.

"I vote we make a quick exit," Djily piped up, scared.

Pierre said, "I'm all for getting out of this creepy place, fast."

"Don't dawdle, everyone," Bacary added, his tone serious. "This building's on its last legs. It feels like it's soaked up years of moisture."

As Bacary spoke, another loud crash echoed from behind, startling everyone.

"Move it, let's go!" Djily shouted.

"The sooner, the better," Pierre agreed.

"Absolutely," Adama muttered in agreement.

They clambered onto the windowsill one after the other, wriggling through the gap between the boards.

Finally, they all stood outside the decrepit house, the storm raging unabated around them.

"Okay, team, let's put as much distance between us and this place as possible," Pierre proposed. "Staying here is a recipe for disaster."

"Or end up haunted," Amath added, his face drained of color. The eerie events they had experienced had clearly shaken him to the core.

Djily nodded in agreement, a hint of unease in his voice. "I'm with you. This place gives me the creeps. Let's get out of here."

Boubou, ever the curious one, stood firm. "I really want to figure out what's up with this house."

Adama, however, was having none of it. "You couldn't pay me enough to go back in there," he declared, almost defiantly. "I say we leave this creepy place. I'm done with it."

"Let's just go," Pierre urged the group. "Staying here is asking for trouble. This old house could collapse on us any minute."

Bouma said, "Plus, there's definitely something off about this place."

Faced with the unanimous decision of the group, Boubou, though reluctantly, agreed to leave. They all made their way to the shed where they had parked their bikes, the rain still pouring down heavily.

"We could wait out the rain in the shed," Boubou suggested, trying to salvage the situation.

"No way," Adama shot back firmly. "I'm getting on my bike and putting as much distance as possible between me and that spooky house. It's really getting to me."

He began to tinker with his bike, getting it ready to leave.

Boubou and Aya, realizing it was pointless to argue, began to prepare for departure along with the others. Silently, they made a pact to return to Kambossa's haunted house as soon as possible to unravel the mystery of the cliffside home.

❖

Before long, the group was on their bikes, pedaling out of the shed and across the yard, heading towards the lane with the rain still pouring around them. At that moment, a creepy laugh echoed from the direction of the house. It was a cold, mocking laugh, cutting through the sound of the storm and the rain's constant drumming on the roof. The loud and taunting laughter lasted for several chilling seconds before stopping suddenly.

The group looked at each other, confused.

"Did you guys just hear someone laughing?" Boubou asked in disbelief.

"Definitely, I heard it!" Djily exclaimed. "That's it for me. I'm out of here."

"That laugh was the creepiest thing I've ever heard," Pierre declared with a shiver. "We need to leave now."

Aya's frustration was evident. "Someone's messing with us! I'm going back there."

"No way, that's not a joke. That place is haunted!" Amath shouted, fear in his voice.

❖

Adam's motorcycle roared to life, and he zoomed down the lane, heading for the main road. Boubou glanced back towards the house, signaling his sister to stick with the group before following Adama. The rest of the gang quickly joined, their bikes racing down the lane.

Behind them, the haunting laughter echoed as if mocking their retreat. But as they pedaled away through the pouring rain, leaving the haunted house hidden among the drenched trees, the sinister laughter gradually faded into silence.

As the group reached the main road, they steered their bikes towards town. The journey was challenging, with the wheels constantly slipping and sliding through the muddy ruts. Soaked to the bone, water streamed from the peaks of their caps right into their eyes. The rain got heavier, blurring their vision to the point where Adam's motorcycle became a faint outline in the misty downpour. He was speeding ahead, making it challenging for the others to keep up.

Aya, riding hard, couldn't shake off her disappointment. She had really wanted to solve the mystery of the cliffside house. She was sure that the creepy shrieks and the mocking laughter weren't supernatural but made by people. Maybe some local kids had been in the house and decided to play a prank on them.

"If that's true," she thought quietly, "everyone at school will have heard the story by Monday. They'll tease us non-stop for running away scared. We should have stayed and investigated."

Boubou, pedaling steadily through the rain, felt differently. The incident with the collapsing ceiling had left a mark on him. They were lucky to have escaped without getting hurt. It could have been a coincidence, but it felt too timely. The memory of the shrieks and that haunting laughter replayed in his mind, sending a chill down his spine. The intensity of it didn't seem like a simple schoolboy joke.

"If that was just some kid, he sure was an amazing actor," Boubou thought to himself, still shaken by the events at the house. "I never really got the whole 'blood running cold' thing until I heard those screams."

Just then, Adam's motorcycle started to act up. It sputtered and jerked, and then, with a loud backfire, the engine died.

"Great timing for a breakdown," Adama grumbled as he got off his bike.

Boubou pulled up next to him, concern on his face. "What's wrong with it?"

"Some issue with the engine," Adama replied, looking it over.

Trying to lighten the mood, Aya joked, "Well, aren't you the lucky one!" She pointed towards an old shed off the side of the road. "There's some cover for you."

Seeing the sense in her suggestion, Adama wheeled his motorcycle towards the shed. Meanwhile, Pierre, realizing the group had stopped, turned his bike around and headed back towards them.

Under the shed's shelter, Adama wrung out his soaked t-shirt and rolled up his sleeves, ready to tackle the bike's problem. Aya, Boubou, and Pierre, relieved to escape the downpour, gathered around to watch or help if they could.

As they huddled in the shed, Bacary's voice echoed through the rain, calling out to them.

"He thinks we're lost," Pierre chuckled. He stepped out to the front of the shed, waving to Bacary. "Hey, over here! Adam's bike broke down!"

Bacary, grumbling about the rain, got off his bike and went to the shed.

Meanwhile, Adama had unscrewed the gas cap of his motorcycle and looked inside. His sudden shout caught everyone's attention. "It's empty!" he blurted out, looking totally confused. I've run out of gas!"

The others gathered closer. "His tank's bone dry," confirmed Bacary, peering over.

"Didn't you fill up back in town?" Boubou asked, puzzled.

"I always fill up before a ride," Adama responded, frustrated. "Someone must have siphoned my gas. But who would do that?"

Boubou, always ready to help, shifted on his bike. "You can ride with me," he offered.

Adama, still processing the situation, snapped the gas cap shut. Then, he exclaimed angrily, "This is ridiculous! First, the Lighthouse thief nabbed my sidecar, and now someone's gone and stolen my gas!"

＊　＊　＊

CHAPTER FOUR

Baywater Pursuit

THE GANG EXCHANGED WORRIED GLANCES, THEIR FACES reflecting a mix of confusion and concern. "I'm positive my tank was full when we left," Adama said, scratching his head.

"So, what do you think happened?" Aya asked, looking around at the group.

"We didn't see anyone near the house," Bacary added, his voice edged with uncertainty.

"And where could they have gone?" Pierre wondered aloud, frowning.

"I told you guys, going to that haunted house was a bad idea. I just knew something was off!" Djily grumbled, crossing his arms.

"It's got to be when we parked the motorcycle in Kambossa's shed, along with all the bikes," Boubou guessed. "Someone must have siphoned the gas then."

"That had to be the moment," Aya agreed firmly. "It was the only time they weren't in our sight."

Adama looked totally confused. "But as Bacary pointed out, there wasn't anyone around," Pierre repeated.

"Maybe not in sight, but someone was there. Remember those creepy screams and that weird laugh? They must've stolen the gas while we were distracted inside the house," Aya reasoned.

"This is starting to feel like some twisted prank," Boubou announced. "We should go back and confront them."

"Not happening," Djily said firmly, shaking his head. "This is getting way too weird for me."

"First, those blood-curdling screams, then the house nearly collapsing on us, and now this? We're lucky we got out of there alive!" Amath added, his voice filled with fear and disbelief.

"And now, we find out your gas is mysteriously missing, taken by some ghostly figure we didn't even see. If I had seen whoever did this, I'd have given them a piece of my mind!" Bouma stated strongly.

"We're better off far from that place," Djily insisted firmly.

The group nodded in agreement, and their decision to avoid the haunted house strengthened.

"I'm telling you, there's something strange about that house. If we keep messing with it, we're asking for trouble," Mohamed added, a worried look on his face.

"But my gas, I need it back!" Adama protested, his frustration evident.

"Wow!" Aya gasped. "Could the gas thief still be lurking in the house?" She ran out of the shed to the road, eyes fixed on the distant house. After a moment, she straightened, breathing a sigh of relief. "Thank goodness our bikes and your motorcycle are still here! Seems like the thief acted alone," Bacary thought out loud.

"I'm heading back there!" Boubou declared, challenging the group.

"Count me in, too!" Aya announced, equally determined.

"If you guys go, you'll have to count me out," Djily interrupted. "You can use my bike to get gas for your bike, Adama. I'll wait here, but there's no way I'm going back into that house."

"Same here," Pierre and Amath said together.

Bouma and Mohamed exchanged uneasy glances.

Boubou and Aya fell silent, torn between their desire to investigate more and keeping their group together. Finally, they decided that staying together was the wiser choice.

"Alright," Boubou said, "Djily's bike is for you, Adama. Djily will ride with Amath. You're too big for either of us to give you a ride back to town. We'll grab some gas, and your problem will be solved before you know it."

Adama approached Djily's bike, looking a bit unsure, sizing up the small bike against his much bigger body. Then, with some maneuvering, Djily managed to get situated behind Amath. Thankfully, the gas was just a minor setback, and a short bike ride should fix their problem. As they got ready to leave, they noticed the rain easing off, turning into a light drizzle by the time they wheeled their bikes out of the shed and onto the road.

"This has been one crazy day," Adama grumbled as he awkwardly got on the tiny bike. "I'm heading back. I have gas at home. We're all soaked—why don't you all come to my place for dinner? What do you say, Boubou, Aya?"

"Thanks for the offer, but we can't. We promised Grandma we'd be home for dinner," Boubou replied.

"I'm taking the side road here. It's a shortcut to our farm," Adama said, pointing to a road splitting off.

The boys set off on their bikes, Adama leading the group. The Diouf siblings followed only until they reached the side road about a hundred meters away. There, they said goodbye to the others, watching Adama lead the group, weighed down by his thoughts, disappearing into the misty road ahead. Boubou and Aya then continued on their way back to town.

The road near the shore dipped and twisted down in a deep spiral along the bay's edge, bringing them close to the cliff top where Kambossa's house was, but now closer to the water. From there, the road gently went down to the shore, running next to the bay towards the city. Boubou glanced up at the massive cliff above them.

Kambossa's place was out of sight, hidden on the high ground and covered by trees, yet its mystery lingered in their minds.

"I really want to go back there," Aya said suddenly. "The mystery of the stolen gas is still bugging me."

"Me too, I'm curious as well. But we should head home like we promised Grandma. We can come back later to investigate," Boubou said reluctantly.

"One moment, I'm sure it's some silly prank. But then, I can't shake this feeling that there's something more, something deeper happening up there," Aya thought, her brow wrinkled in concentration. She was having strange feelings, almost as if someone was talking to her in her mind. She suspected it was her father, a hint that she might have inherited her Grandma's psychic abilities. Curiosity nudged her to try the cowry shells in her pocket, but she wasn't quite ready to tell Boubou about this new skill.

"There definitely were a bunch of weird things happening at that house. I can still hear those creepy screams in my head," Boubou said, shivering slightly.

"Yeah, I guess you're right. We should head back. But I really want to figure out what's actually going on there," Aya responded, her curiosity as strong as ever.

"Whoever took the gas did it quickly. We weren't away from the bikes for too long," Boubou pointed out.

"It definitely rules out any ghostly explanations," Aya chuckled.

"I never believed that ghost story. It was a person who siphoned the gas. And they must have been spying on us, saw us put the bikes away, and took their chance while we were inside the house," Boubou guessed.

"Unless the gas was taken before we even reached the house when we left the bikes under those trees for a bit?" Aya wondered.

"No, that wouldn't have given them enough time. We barely stepped into the front room before those screams made us all run back out. It had to be when the bikes were in the shed," Boubou said confidently.

The rain had stopped as they continued their ride, but the wet road was slippery. They focused on steering down the steep path toward the bay, concentrating on not skidding. It was when they reached the flatter, safer road along the shore that they started talking again.

❖

Suddenly, Boubou and Aya noticed a dramatic scene happening in the bay below them. Their hearts raced as they watched an intense chase on the water. From where they were, they could see two motorboats racing across the waves. With only one person in it, the first boat seemed desperate to get away, making sharp, unpredictable turns. The second boat was relentless, getting closer and closer with each passing second.

"It's like something out of a movie," Aya whispered, her eyes wide with surprise.

On the second boat, a figure stood with a rifle, aiming at the fleeing boat. The roar of the engines and the occasional crack of gunfire echoed across the bay, making the scene even more tense.

"Look, they're almost catching up!" Boubou pointed out anxiously.

The figure on the chasing boat fired again, the shot ringing through the air. The siblings held their breath as they watched the bullet's path, trying hard to see if it hit its target.

"I can't tell if he hit him," Aya said, squinting her eyes to get a clearer view.

The lone man in the lead boat ducked low, either to avoid the gunfire or because he was hit. Despite this, his boat didn't slow down; it kept plowing through the waves like an unmanned missile on a dangerous course.

The chase neared its end as the two boats got dangerously close, almost side by side. Boubou and Aya could hardly believe what they were seeing. The tension was so thick that it seemed like the boats might crash or the man being chased might do something desperate.

"What do we do?" Aya asked, her voice shaking slightly. "Should we call for help?"

Before Boubou could answer, the scene reached its critical point. Now almost touching, the two boats were engaged in a high-speed dance of danger and desperation. The siblings could only watch, hoping for the best but fearing the worst. Suddenly, the first boat exploded, sending a fiery plume into the sky.

CHAPTER FIVE

Peril In The Waters

THE MAN FROM THE FIRST BOAT THRASHED IN THE WATER, struggling to stay afloat amidst the wreckage. His desperate cries for help pierced the air, jolting Boubou and Aya out of their stunned silence.

"We have to help him!" Aya shouted, scanning the area for a way to get down to the shore quickly.

Boubou spotted a rowboat partially hidden in a cove at the base of the cliff. "Over there!" he pointed. "We can use that boat!"

They scrambled down the rocky slope, determined to save the man fueling their steps. The path was dangerous, but they reached the bottom without incident and found the rowboat. It was old and weather-beaten but seemed seaworthy.

"Let's get it into the water!" urged Boubou.

Together, they dragged the boat over the pebbles, its keel scraping noisily against the shingle. Hastily, they fitted the oars into the oarlocks and climbed aboard.

Rowing hard, they made their way towards the man in the bay, who had now noticed them and was shouting for them to hurry. His cries soon stopped as he lost strength, and for a moment, Boubou feared the worst. Fortunately, the man was still visible, clinging desperately to his fragment of wreckage.

Behind them, the motorboat was an inferno, flames leaping skyward. Thick smoke billowed up, a dark pillar against the sky. The other motorboat's engine echoed across the bay as it sped away, its silhouette fading into the mist.

Their focus now was solely on the rescue. Determined and skilled at rowing, Boubou and Aya propelled the rowboat with impressive speed, each stroke bringing them closer to the desperate man. Their coordination was perfect, a testament to their skill and urgency.

Just a few meters away, Boubou turned to offer a shout of encouragement, but his heart skipped a beat. Overcome with exhaustion, the man released his hold on the debris and disappeared beneath the water's surface.

"He's drowning, Aya!" Boubou yelled, panic in his voice.

Without a second thought, he tossed his oar into the boat and dove into the water, swimming powerfully. Aya's cry of alarm rang out as she watched her brother's daring plunge.

"Hold on!" she shouted, guiding the boat closer.

Boubou reached the spot, diving into the murky depths. The water was dark, but his determination pushed him forward. His hand brushed against the fabric, pulling the man towards him with all his strength.

Breaking the surface, Boubou gasped for air, the unconscious man in tow. "I've got him!" he called out.

Aya rowed furiously, bringing the boat alongside them. With immense effort, they hauled the man into the boat, his limp body heavy and unresponsive.

"He's not breathing!" Aya cried.

"Start CPR," Boubou instructed, climbing back into the boat. "I'll row us to shore."

Aya began chest compressions, her voice steady and rhythmic as she counted. After what felt like an eternity, the man coughed, water spluttering from his mouth. Aya let out a relieved cry as he took a shaky breath.

"He's alive!" Aya exclaimed, tears of relief in her eyes.

Boubou rowed with all his might, the shoreline drawing closer with each stroke. Finally, they felt the satisfying crunch of pebbles beneath the boat's keel. Boubou jumped out, pulling the boat partially onto the shore. Together, they carefully lifted the man and carried him towards the salt farmhouse.

Navigating a path that meandered through the salt ponds to the back of the house, they managed to transport the man's limp form despite its weight and the challenge of the terrain. As they approached, a tall woman with a kind, weathered face hurried out from the house, her expression turning to one of concern. A man wearing overalls, clearly a salt farmer, emerged from a nearby salt pond. Both the salt farmer and his wife had spotted the siblings' approach.

"My goodness, what in the world happened?" the woman exclaimed, her eyes widening at the sight.

"He was nearly drowning in the bay," Boubou explained quickly. "We saw your house and—"

"Bring him inside," the salt farmer interrupted with a deep voice, his tone firm yet concerned.

The woman, moving swiftly, held the door open for them. With the farmer's help, Boubou and Aya carried the unconscious man into the house, laying him gently on a couch in the living room.

The cozy and well-furnished room was warm and welcoming, a stark contrast to the critical situation they were dealing with. The farmer's wife eyed the puddle forming under the man, a flash of distress momentarily crossing her face for her freshly scrubbed floor.

However, the situation's urgency pushed her to the kitchen to find something to help revive the stranger.

In this unfamiliar yet welcoming home, the siblings waited anxiously, hoping that their efforts would be enough to save the man's life.

"Rub his hands; that'll help bring some color back to his face," the salt farmer, a big man with a black beard, commanded authoritatively. "And let's get those boots off. We can wrap his feet in warm flannel."

For the next few minutes, the house was abuzz with lifesaving activity. The salt farmer and his wife moved with a sense of urgency while Boubou and Aya diligently massaged the stranger's hands and feet, hoping to stir him back to consciousness. Gradually, their efforts began to show results.

The man on the couch started to show signs of life, stirring weakly. His eyelids fluttered, and his lips moved silently. Then, finally, his eyes opened, his gaze unfocused and confused.

"Where am I?" he whispered with a feeble voice.

"You're safe," Boubou reassured him. "You're among friends now."

"Pretty—close to—gone, wasn't I?" the stranger murmured.

"Yeah, it was a close call. You were engulfed by flames, and you almost drowned," said Aya.

"But you're okay now," Boubou responded, his voice steady and comforting.

"It was Scorpion," the stranger rasped, his voice a haunting whisper that seemed to echo through the room. His eyes, wide with fear and realization, locked onto an unseen horizon. "Scorpion betrayed me—the treacherous viper!"

✳ ✳ ✳

CHAPTER SIX

Scorpion

THE NAME "SCORPION" HUNG IN THE AIR, LEAVING THE DIOUF siblings and their hosts with more questions than answers about the stranger's ordeal and the events that had led to his near-fatal state. This unexpected statement surprised everyone, adding a new layer of mystery to the already dramatic situation.

At that moment, the salt farmer's wife, Mariama, entered the room, carrying a soothing remedy of hot ginger water. The man on the couch eagerly accepted the drink, drinking it with apparent gratitude.

"We should get him settled in the spare room," the salt farmer decided, glancing at the exhausted stranger. "A warm bed is what he needs most right now. I'll take care of him, but I'll need these kids to lend a hand."

The stranger's voice, weak and hoarse, suddenly broke the silence. "I think... I was shot," he murmured, his hand feebly gesturing towards his side.

Aya, looking concerned, leaned in closer to check. "There's blood on his coat!" she announced, her voice tinged with alarm.

Upon closer examination, they found the stranger's claim to be valid. A bullet wound marked his right side. Thankfully, it seemed to be a superficial flesh wound, but it had bled quite a bit, leaving the man visibly drained and weakened.

With the utmost care, Boubou and Aya helped remove the injured man's clothing, revealing the extent of his wound. The salt farmer gently cleaned the wound with a basin of warm salt water and a clean sponge. The bullet had torn through the man's coat, searing a path across his torso. As the farmer applied salt to the injury, the stranger clenched his teeth, enduring the sharp sting of pain.

"Salt water will help clean it and promote healing," said the salt farmer.

Boubou, remembering his school lessons on osmosis, knew he was right. This process would draw out fluids and bacteria, helping the wound's natural healing. Finally, he wrapped the wound in clean bandages, securing them carefully.

"Now, let's get him to bed. Are you able to walk?" the farmer asked, turning his attention to the wounded man.

With a strained effort, the man tried to rise from the couch, but he collapsed back down, his strength failing him.

"I'm afraid—I can't make it," he admitted, his voice weakened with the effort.

"Alright then, we'll help carry you. Kids, lend me a hand here," the farmer instructed, signaling to Boubou and Aya.

Together, they prepared to carefully lift the wounded man. They helped the salt farmer carry him upstairs to a simple, cozy room. They settled him into the bed and tucked him under warm blankets. The man sighed deeply and closed his eyes, a sign of relief and exhaustion.

"He's mostly weak from blood loss," the salt farmer observed as they stood by the bed. "A deep sleep will do him good."

❖

Leaving the man to rest, they all moved to the kitchen, where the Diouf siblings recounted their exciting adventures. The salt farmer listened intently, his expression thoughtful.

"Strange business, this," he finally said, turning to his wife, Mariama. "What do you think?"

Mariama nodded in agreement with her husband, Boubacar. "Seems like another smuggling mishap to me," she guessed.

Boubacar nodded, his face reflecting concern and acknowledgment. "Yes, it does seem likely to be something like that."

"Smuggling!" Boubou said, surprised.

"Yes, smuggling. There's been quite a bit of it around Zinguichou Bay recently," the salt farmer explained. "I've had my suspicions for a while. There are too many motorboats out there, especially at night. If it's not smuggling, it's something else illegal."

"Do you think this guy might've been shot over a smuggling fight?" Boubou asked, curious about the possibility.

The salt farmer gave a shrug. "Could be, could be. I can't say for sure, and it's risky to guess without solid facts. But it wouldn't surprise me."

The salt farmers, who introduced themselves as Mr. and Mrs. Touma, were just about to have dinner and warmly invited the Diouf siblings to join them.

Boubou turned to Mr. Touma, a hint of concern in his voice. "Do you have a phone we could use? We need to call our grandma. She should know we'll be staying here for dinner." He paused, feeling the weight of the day's events on their shoulders.

"You'll need to explain everything to her later, of course," Mrs. Touma replied.

After getting permission to use the phone, Boubou quickly dialed their grandma, his voice steady but tired. Their grandma, always trusting and understanding, agreed without asking too many questions. She knew they were safe and would share their story in due time. Her calm acceptance comforted Boubou and Aya in the midst of an otherwise chaotic day.

After the morning's events, Boubou and Aya were both exhausted and hungry, and they gratefully accepted the invitation.

They settled into their seats at the dining table, ready for a meal that, while simple, was hearty and filling. The food consisted of a homestyle chicken dish and savory baked beans, enhanced by the comforting smell of freshly brewed tea. The conversation naturally drifted to the day's strange events out on the bay as they ate.

Boubou and Aya, however, carefully avoided mentioning their encounter at Kambossa's place. They remembered the valuable lesson that a good Detective should always listen more than they speak, a principle they decided to follow. After all, discussing one mystery at dinner seemed sufficient.

❖

After the meal, as Mr. Touma leaned back in his chair, enjoying his pipe, Boubou wanted to dig deeper into the mystery. "I really want to learn more about this whole thing," he said thoughtfully. "Maybe the man has woken up by now."

"It's worth checking," Mr. Touma replied, puffing on his pipe. "You could try asking him a few questions. I'm just as curious as you are."

❖

They made their way upstairs to the spare room. The stranger was sleeping, but the creak of the door and their soft footsteps woke him up. He opened his eyes slowly, looking at them with a dazed expression. The mood in the room shifted slightly, curiosity and questions hanging in the air.

"Feeling any better?" Boubou asked, his tone gentle.

"Oh, yes," the stranger responded weakly, the effort of speaking clear. "I must have lost quite a bit of blood, though."

"That happened when they shot at you right before your boat exploded," Aya added, trying to piece together the events.

The man in the bed nodded a silent acknowledgment but offered no more information.

"What's your name?" Mr. Touma asked directly, getting to the point.

There was a brief pause before the man replied, "Hounsou."

The response seemed evasive, almost rehearsed, causing Boubou and Aya to exchange knowing looks. Even Mr. Touma seemed skeptical, scratching his chin in thought.

"And how did you end up in this situation, Mr. Hounsou? Why were they shooting at you?" Mr. Touma pressed on, wondering.

"Please, don't ask me," the man pleaded. "I can't tell you anything."

"I suppose you know that these young folks here saved your life?" the salt farmer pointed out, directing Hounsou's attention to Boubou and Aya.

"Yes, I know, and I'm very grateful for that," Hounsou acknowledged, his voice showing genuine appreciation. "But please, don't ask me any questions. I can't tell you anything about what happened."

"Not even to them, after they've saved your life?" the farmer pressed, confused by Hounsou's reluctance.

Hounsou, however, remained firm, shaking his head with a stubborn resolve. "I can't explain any of it. Please, just leave me to rest."

The room fell into an uneasy silence, the air thick with unanswered questions and the mystery surrounding Hounsou's enigmatic figure.

Understanding that further questioning would lead nowhere, Boubou and Aya gestured to the salt farmer, signaling it was time to leave Hounsou in peace. Quietly, they left the room, gently closing the door behind them.

Once downstairs, the farmer couldn't hide his frustration. "I'll be darned! That's the most tight-lipped young man I've ever come across," he muttered. "Here you two go saving his life, and he won't even say why he was tearing across the bay in a motorboat with people shooting at him."

Boubou thought about the situation carefully. "He must have his reasons. It's his business, and we can't force him to share," Boubou said. "Maybe in time, he'll feel comfortable enough to explain." Despite the mystery and their natural curiosity, Boubou knew respecting Hounsou's privacy was important.

"He's involved with those smugglers; that's my guess," Mr. Touma said with conviction.

"We should probably head back home," Boubou suggested, considering the time. "Do you mind keeping him here a bit longer? We could arrange to have him moved to a hospital later."

Mr. Touma shook his head firmly. "Smuggler or not, he's not leaving this house until he's recovered. No one will ever say Boubacar Touma turned away a sick man. He stays here until he's well."

"We'll come back in a day or two to check on him," Aya added, appreciating the salt farmer's kindness.

"He'll be well taken care of, no matter what he's involved in. Mariama and I will see to that," the farmer assured them.

After securing the rowboat back at its mooring place, Boubou and Aya said goodbye to the kind-hearted salt farmer and his wife. They then made their way to where they had left their bikes. Soon, they were cycling back toward town, their minds filled with the day's events and the mystery surrounding the stranger they had saved.

As they pedaled back home, Aya couldn't help but comment on the day's events. "That guy is strange," she remarked, thinking about the stranger's behavior and the mysterious situation.

Boubou nodded in agreement, his thoughts mirroring his sister's. "Definitely weird," he said. "Something's unusual about this whole thing. We can't ignore it."

Their conversation was filled with guesses and curiosity, the day's mystery lingering in their minds as they continued their journey home.

❖

Upon arriving home in the mid-afternoon, Boubou and Aya parked their bikes in the garage before heading into the house. They found their grandma in what used to be their dad's library. As Boubou and Aya entered the room, their grandma looked up from her book with an expectant smile, clearly waiting for the story they had promised to share over the phone. She set her book aside and reclined comfortably in her chair, her eyes sparkling with curiosity.

"So, tell me about your adventures today," she encouraged, her tone warm and inviting, eager to hear the details of their promised story.

"We've had quite the adventure today, Grandma," Boubou began, his tone hinting at the excitement of the day's events. "We went to the old Kambossa's place with some friends."

"Ah, the haunted house, right? Did you see any ghosts?" Grandma Diouf asked, her voice playful and skeptical.

Exchanging glances, Aya replied, "Well, we didn't exactly see any ghosts, but—"

"You're not about to tell me you heard some, are you?" Grandma Diouf interrupted, her laughter ringing out in delight at the thought.

"You might find it funny, but strange things happened out there," Aya insisted, her expression serious, hinting their story was more than just a playful ghost tale.

Boubou and Aya shared the details of their unusual experiences at Kambossa's house. They recounted each event carefully, from the eerie moments in the haunted house to the dramatic rescue in the bay.

However, Grandma Diouf, upon hearing their tale, remained skeptical. "It sounds like a prank from some of your school friends," she remarked dismissively. "I bet they're having a good laugh about it right now."

"But Grandma, how do you explain the gas being siphoned from the bikes?" Boubou asked, puzzled by her casual dismissal and trying to underline the seriousness of their adventure.

"They probably just siphoned the gas to add a bit of mystery to their joke," she suggested. "I wouldn't be surprised if they return it to you at school on Monday just to show they were behind it all along."

Grandma Diouf's reasoning seemed possible to the siblings, and they exchanged glances, feeling slightly embarrassed at the thought of having been tricked by a prank. The idea that their friends might have planned the gas siphoning as part of a bigger joke was something they hadn't considered.

"Geez, we'll be teased non-stop at school if that's true," Aya sighed, accepting the possibility with a sense of resignation. "Well, we might as well brace ourselves for it. But that's not all that happened. Wait until you hear about our way home. Go on, Boubou, tell her."

"Another adventure?" Grandma Diouf asked, her interest sparked once again.

"Yes, a real one this time, no jokes involved," Boubou affirmed.

He then began recounting the intense episode with the two motorboats in Zinguichou Bay—the thrilling chase, the dramatic explosion, and their brave rescue of the injured man. Boubou downplayed their heroism in the rescue, but as the story unfolded, Grandma Diouf listened more and more intently, nodding her head in approval and satisfaction at their bravery and quick thinking. The seriousness and reality of this adventure were apparent, and it was evident that this was no schoolyard prank.

"Good work! Good work!" Grandma Diouf praised, her tone a mix of admiration and concern. "You definitely saved that man's life, and it sounds like you've uncovered something quite mysterious with that motorboat chase. What did the man say his name was?"

"Hounsou," Boubou replied, his tone indicating his uncertainty about the name's authenticity.

Grandma Diouf's eyebrows arched in mild surprise. "Hounsou, huh? It's a name that is common enough around Africa; it could be real. But it sounds like he might be hiding something. Did he give you any reason for the chase? What did he say when you asked him?"

"He wouldn't tell us anything," Boubou admitted. "We tried asking him a few questions, but he said he couldn't explain."

"That makes it all the more mysterious," Grandma Diouf thought carefully. "Do you think he might open up once he recovers a bit more?"

"I'm afraid he won't be too forthcoming," Boubou replied, his voice reflecting his skepticism about the man's willingness to share any information. "He seemed pretty determined to keep quiet about himself and the people chasing him."

Suddenly, Aya chimed in with a spark of recollection. "Remember, Boubou? When we first brought him into the house and he came to? What did he say?"

"Oh, right! I almost forgot about that," Boubou said, recalling the moment. "He muttered something like, 'Scorpion got me, the treacherous viper.' I didn't know what to make of it at the time."

"Scorpion!" Grandma Diouf exclaimed, her interest visibly heightened as she sat up straighter. "Are you sure he said Scorpion? That was the name?"

Boubou nodded, "Absolutely, I'm sure of it. You remember it too, right, Aya?"

"Yes, he definitely said Scorpion," Aya confirmed.

"Well, that does give us a lead," Grandma Diouf mused thoughtfully. "You might not know about Scorpion, but I do."

Astounded by their grandma's knowledge, Boubou and Aya listened intently as she spoke of their late dad's familiarity with the name 'Scorpion.'

"I heard your father mention 'Scorpion' several times," Grandma Diouf revealed.

"Who is he?" Boubou asked, eager for more information.

"Scorpion is known to be involved in various criminal activities across West Africa," Grandma Diouf explained. "Your father had some dealings with him during his investigations. He always said Scorpion was dangerous and cunning, a master of deception."

Aya's eyes lit up with a sudden idea. "Let's use the cowrie shells to ask Dad for help!" she suggested excitedly.

Understanding her grandchildren's desire for answers, Grandma Diouf gave a knowing wink. She stood up to retrieve the cowrie shells, an ancient tool for spiritual communication.

❖

They gathered together in the living room, settling into their usual circle with excitement in the air. The room seemed to hum with hope and eagerness as they prepared to connect with the spiritual world, seeking insights only their late dad, a skilled Detective, could provide.

With practiced hands, Grandma Diouf began to arrange and manipulate the cowrie shells. A calm focus filled the room as she delved deeper into the spiritual connection. The shells clinked softly, each movement bringing them closer to the otherworldly wisdom they sought. After a moment of deep concentration, Grandma Diouf began to speak, her voice carrying the guidance they sought from beyond.

"Your father knows a lot about the Scorpion," she conveyed, her words carrying the weight of their dad's deep understanding and knowledge. "Your father says that the Scorpion is a notorious criminal," she relayed, her voice steady but filled with a newfound seriousness. "He's a key figure in a blood diamonds smuggling network, responsible for stealing and exporting these raw diamonds from the African mines. Could he be using Zinguichou Bay as an exit point for these activities?"

"What are blood diamonds?" Aya asked.

"Blood diamonds, Aya, are precious stones mined in war zones and sold to finance conflicts, often involving terrible human rights abuses," Boubou explained, his tone serious. "They're dug up in African countries where civil wars and fights for control are common. The people who mine these diamonds are usually forced to work under brutal conditions, and the profits from selling these diamonds often go to warlords and rebel groups. So when they say 'blood diamonds,' it's because the cost of these gems isn't just their market price—it's the suffering and bloodshed of innocent people."

Boubou and Aya exchanged a look of concern. The puzzle pieces began coming together, hinting at a much larger and more dangerous situation than they had initially realized.

55

* * *

CHAPTER SEVEN

Tied Secrets

Channeled through the cowries, the revelation from their late dad's spirit left Boubou and Aya surprised and deep in thought. Grandma Diouf, her movements with the cowries fluid and practiced, leaned in, indicating there was more to come from her son's spirit, the seasoned Detective.

"You might have uncovered something significant," she said in a hushed, serious tone. "Your father stresses the importance of being discreet. If The Scorpion is indeed active in this area, capturing him could be a significant achievement."

Boubou thought out loud, "The Scorpion is a weird name. It sounds like a nickname."

"And remember, the salt farmer mentioned smuggling activities in the Bay," Aya added, connecting the dots.

Grandma Diouf's voice, still conveying the insights from the spiritual realm, continued, "Your father acknowledges that smuggling has always been a part of Zinguichou Bay, though historically on a smaller scale. However, the Scorpion and his group are involved in large-scale international blood diamond smuggling. He was last known to be active on the south coast but likely shifted operations due to increased heat. It appears he's been off the radar for the past year or so."

This information painted a picture of a larger, more dangerous criminal operation possibly unfolding in their own backyard, far beyond the scale of local petty smuggling they had imagined.

"Maybe this Hounsou at the salt farm will open up eventually," Boubou mused.

"Let's tell Dad we're planning to interview him," Aya suggested eagerly. "But we'll wait a few days. Give him time to recover."

Boubou, always cautious, added, "This really falls under the jurisdiction of the Zinguichou authorities. Since we're not officially involved, we have to be careful. But we might still gather some useful information to help them."

"We'll check on him tomorrow and see how he's doing," Aya decided.

Grandma Diouf, expertly manipulating the cowries, conveyed their plan. "Proceed with your visit," she advised, relaying their dad's wisdom. "But remember, don't ask direct questions. Don't raise any suspicions. And above all, be careful. Don't take any risks."

"That's good advice," Aya agreed. "If he thinks we're onto him, he might try to disappear, and we could lose any lead on him."

Grandma continued, "Since you saved his life, he owes you a debt of gratitude. It will seem natural for you to return to check on him." Their late dad's guidance through the cowries provided a strategic approach for their next visit, balancing their curiosity with the need to maintain Hounsou's trust.

"If he seems to be recovering quickly, we can ask the salt farmer to let us know. Then we can go and talk to him right away," Boubou reasoned. "If it looks like he'll be there for a while, we can wait until he's feeling better."

Thinking of another angle, Aya suggested, "Maybe he's a Detective himself."

"That thought crossed my mind, too," Boubou admitted.

As Grandma Diouf continued her work with the cowries, another message appeared. "It's possible he's a Secret Service agent who stumbled upon Scorpion's operations and got shot because of it," she relayed.

"That would make sense as to why he wouldn't share any details about himself," Boubou said.

"But we shouldn't rule out the chance that he's an enemy of Scorpion. If that's the case, he might eventually be willing to talk to us," Aya added optimistically.

The siblings continued asking their dad more questions through Grandma and the cowries, but no significant insights emerged. Nonetheless, they decided to visit the Touma salt farm the next day, Sunday, to check on the condition of the mysterious Mr. Hounsou and possibly gather more clues about the unfolding mystery.

The clairvoyant session with their dad's spirit through the cowries ended, leaving Boubou and Aya with much to think about. The rest of the evening was spent in the warm company of their grandma, immersed in deep discussion and speculation about the day's mysterious events. The holiday had turned out to be far more eventful than any of them had anticipated.

As they revisited each detail of their adventure, they tried to piece together the puzzle of what had happened in Zinguichou Bay. Despite their best efforts and the insights gained from their late dad's spirit, a straightforward solution to the mystery eluded them. The mystery seemed to deepen with each discussion, leaving more questions than answers.

Regarding the eerie occurrences at the old fisherman's house perched on the cliff, they gradually began to lean towards accepting Grandma Diouf's suggestion. It seemed increasingly likely that their initial frightful experience resulted from a well-crafted prank by someone with a taste for mischief. Yet, even with this potential explanation, a part of the mystery remained, wrapped in the shadows of the bay and the elusive figure known as the Scorpion.

The next morning, after a big breakfast, Boubou and Aya spent time cleaning their bikes. Yesterday's storm had left them covered in mud and dirt, but the brother and sister worked hard to make them shiny again. Once the bikes were sparkling like new, they rolled them out of the garage, all set for their trip to the Touma salt farm. They couldn't wait to see how the man they had courageously saved was doing.

As they got ready to go, Boubou reminded his sister about the advice their dad had given them before he passed away. "Don't forget what Dad said!" he warned. "We have to be careful not to ask him too many questions. We don't want him to get suspicious. The main thing we need to find out is how long he's planning to stay at the salt farm. If he's not badly hurt, he might leave soon, and we need to know that."

Aya agreed, promising to follow the guidance they had received through the cowrie shells. They both knew the importance of being thoughtful and respectful in this situation. With their father's wise words in their hearts, they headed off to the Touma salt farm, feeling a mix of curiosity and determination.

The brother and sister enjoyed the beautiful Sunday weather, utterly different from the rainy day before. The recent rain had settled the dust, making their bike ride along the shore road much nicer.

As they pedaled, Aya couldn't help but share a worry. "What if Mr. Hounsou leaves before we get there? That would be really disappointing."

Boubou, on the other hand, seemed hopeful. "I don't think he's going anywhere anytime soon. That wound on his side looked bad enough to keep him in bed for a while. Plus, he lost a lot of blood… he'll need time to get better."

"I just hope he's not a Detective," Aya said thoughtfully.

"Why's that?" Boubou asked, looking at her.

"Well, it would be really exciting if we could actually help with this case. If The Scorpion is around here and the local police don't know about him yet, we could make a big difference," Aya explained, her eyes shining excitedly.

"It would be an amazing chance," Boubou agreed. "But I have a feeling that Hounsou might be a Detective. If that's true, then finding out anything definite about him could be tough. Why else would Scorpion's men go after him so hard? They clearly thought they had taken care of him."

"Or he could be another smuggler they wanted to get rid of," Aya suggested, thinking of another possibility.

"Maybe," Boubou admitted. "But my guess is he's more likely working in law enforcement, maybe even Secret Service."

As they approached the Touma salt farm, the mystery of Mr. Hounsou and how he was connected to The Scorpion kept swirling in their minds.

❖

When Boubou and Aya reached the lane leading to the salt farm, they noticed how quiet everything was, which made them feel a little uneasy. The salt ponds were still, the shed was empty, and the house looked deserted. The closed doors on such a warm day just made the whole scene seem even stranger.

"This is weird," Boubou said, parking their bikes under a big tree near the back of the house. "Do you think Mr. and Mrs. Touma went out and left Hounsou by himself?"

Feeling curious and worried, they knocked on the front door, but nobody answered.

"Let's try the back," Aya suggested, leading the way around the house.

Their knocks at the back door also went unanswered, making the mystery even bigger. "They must be out," Aya said, sounding confused.

"But what about Hounsou? They wouldn't just leave him here, especially since he's hurt," Boubou thought out loud, his forehead wrinkled as he tried to figure it out.

They knocked on the back door repeatedly, but no one answered. Boubou carefully tried the doorknob and, to their surprise, found that it was unlocked and opened easily.

"Well, they didn't lock the place up, at least," Boubou noted, feeling cautious. "Let's go in. If Hounsou is still upstairs, we can check on him. I'm sure Mr. Touma won't mind, especially with everything that's happened. They probably didn't expect anyone to visit today."

With a quick nod to each other, the brother and sister stepped inside, being very careful.

Boubou and Aya stood in shocked silence as they looked at the messy kitchen scene. It was completely different from the neat and clean room they remembered from yesterday. The mess was scary: kitchen stuff was thrown around, furniture was knocked over, and broken dishes were all over the floor. It was obvious that something violent and unexpected had happened. The quiet house made the mystery feel even more significant.

"What in the world happened here?" Boubou shouted, sounding both shocked and confused.

"It looks like a tornado hit this place," Aya added, her eyes wide as she took in the scene.

"There must have been some kind of fight or struggle," Boubou figured out, his mind racing with ideas. "We need to check the rest of the house right now."

They moved carefully, knowing they were going into someone else's house. Still, they also had to make sure Hounsou was okay and find more clues about the confusing events they had gotten mixed up in.

Quickly, they went to the next room, where they saw something even more shocking. Mr. and Mrs. Touma were sitting in the middle of the room, but they were in a really upsetting situation. The couple was tied up and gagged, unable to move or speak, their faces filled with fear and confusion.

CHAPTER EIGHT

Witness Without A Trace

BOUBOU AND AYA JUMPED INTO ACTION, QUICKLY WORKING to untie Mr. and Mrs. Touma. The ropes tying up the salt farmer and his wife were tight and secure, clearly showing that whoever did this wanted to make sure they couldn't get free on their own. Even though it was tough, the brother and sister loosened the knots and removed the gags quickly.

"Thank goodness!" Mrs. Touma gasped, her voice a mix of relief and upset, as Aya gently pulled the gag away. Mr. Touma, visibly shaken and angry about what had happened, quickly stood up and threw the ropes away with force.

"What happened here?" Boubou and Aya asked simultaneously, their faces filled with worry and confusion.

The Toumas struggled to collect their thoughts for a moment, clearly overwhelmed by the scary event. Finally, Mr. Touma, getting some of his composure back, limped to the window and pointed down the shore road, his hand shaking.

Feeling the need to act fast, Boubou and Aya quickly listened to the farmer's first words. "They went that way! Down the shore road," Mr. Touma shouted, his voice shaking with anger and desperation.

"They kidnapped Hounsou?" Aya repeated in shock, her mind racing.

"Yes," Mr. Touma confirmed, his voice strained. "Four men, armed and dangerous. They barged in, overpowered us, and then went upstairs for Hounsou. They just threw him into a car and sped off."

"Four men…" Boubou repeated, already thinking about going after them.

"How long ago did they leave?" he asked urgently.

"Not more than ten minutes," Mr. Touma replied, clearly agitated. "You might have caught them if you'd arrived a bit sooner."

Without hesitation, Boubou turned to Aya. "Let's go, Aya! We might still catch them if we hurry. They can't be too far ahead."

With a shared sense of purpose, the brother and sister rushed out of the house and back to their bikes. The seriousness of the situation was clear—they had a chance to track down Hounsou's kidnappers and possibly uncover a more extensive criminal operation. Time was crucial, and every second counted as they started a chase that could lead them into unknown dangers.

Aya jumped into action alongside her brother, both feeling determined and knowing they had to act fast. The brother and sister quickly left Mr. and Mrs. Touma in the farmhouse, taking care of their sore wrists and ankles, and dashed outside. They were on their bikes in no time, the chains clicking in a steady rhythm as they pedaled as fast as they could down the lane, weaving past the salt ponds and onto the shore road.

"This is a really bold move," Boubou shouted over the noise of their quick movement.

"Those crooks belong in jail," Aya replied, her voice strong and determined.

As they raced in the direction Mr. Touma had pointed, Boubou suddenly remembered seeing a cloud of dust kicked up by a speeding car on the main road just before arriving at the salt farm. He hadn't thought much of it at the time since vehicles were common on Sundays, but now he realized it could have been the kidnappers.

"If only we had been here a little earlier," he said, disappointed.

Aya, however, was hopeful. "We can still catch them. They don't have too much of a head start. Maybe we can follow them to a town and get the police to arrest all of them."

The Diouf siblings pushed their bikes to the limit, racing along the road to catch the kidnappers. Their knowledge of the area, gained from countless rides on the region's challenging dirt tracks and cliffside paths, helped them in this urgent chase. For a while, Boubou managed to follow the car by tracking the distinct tread marks it left in the dust. However, the trail became hard to follow at the intersection with the road leading to the Sambou farm, where tire tracks from another vehicle had covered up the path of the car they were chasing.

They sped past the lane leading to Kambossa's place, continuing their pursuit along the shore road until they reached a hilltop that gave them a wide view of the surrounding area. From this high point, they could see the road stretch out for over half a mile, eventually disappearing into a grove of trees. Despite their efforts, there was no sign of the car they were chasing.

"They've managed to get away from us," Boubou said, sounding slightly disappointed as he slowed his bike to a stop.

"They had quite a head start, and they were moving fast," Aya added, her voice showing a mix of frustration and acceptance. "Should we keep going?"

Boubou thought for a moment before replying, "I don't think there's much point in continuing. Let's head back to the salt farm. We need to find out more from Mr. and Mrs. Touma about what happened."

With that decision made, the brother and sister turned their bikes around. They started the ride back to the salt farm, their minds full of questions and the hope that the Toumas could give them more information about the confusing situation.

❖

As they pedaled back toward the farm, Boubou and Aya were deep in thought about the mysterious kidnapping.

"It seems like those men in the other boat either saw us saving Hounsou or found out he was at the farmhouse," Aya guessed, her voice showing concern and a hint of fear. "They must be pretty desperate to go this far."

Boubou, cycling alongside her, had a severe look on his face. "I'm really worried about what might happen to Hounsou now. They already tried to kill him once. This time—"

"Do you think they might actually kill him?" Aya asked, her voice shaking.

Boubou sighed. "It's a scary thought, but they showed no mercy out in the bay. They left him for dead then. It's possible they might try to finish the job."

Aya shuddered at the thought but then argued, "If they wanted to kill him, why go through all the trouble of kidnapping him? Maybe they just want to keep him quiet. They might be worried he could tell people about them chasing him and setting his motorboat on fire."

"They were clearly desperate to get Hounsou," Boubou thought as they rode. "To barge into the house in the middle of the day, tie up Mr. and Mrs. Touma... it's a bold move. We were lucky to have arrived when we did. They could have been left tied up and helpless for hours."

When they returned to the salt farm, Boubou and Aya found the Toumas still visibly shaken but starting to recover from the scary experience. Mrs. Touma, despite what had just happened, had already begun to clean up the mess left by the intruders and put her house back in order.

"We couldn't catch them," Boubou told Mr. Touma, his voice heavy with disappointment.

Mr. Touma nodded, his expression resigned. "I didn't think you would. They were in a hurry to leave, and with that fancy car of theirs... But I had hoped you might."

Boubou asked for more details. "You mentioned there were four of them. What did they look like? Can you describe them?"

"The whole thing happened so fast. One of the men, tall with a thin face, came to the door. He claimed he was the brother of the man we'd rescued and said he came to take him away. I got suspicious and asked for his name. But as I was talking to him outside, someone attacked me from behind. I tried to fight back, but more men appeared from around the corner of the house, where they'd been hiding, and overpowered me. The next thing I knew, my wife and I were tied up and left in the living room while they went upstairs for Hounsou."

Boubou, wanting to understand everything that happened, asked, "Did Hounsou try to fight back when they took him?"

"He did," Mr. Touma replied, feeling regretful. "He shouted for help, but I was helpless, and he was too weak to put up much of a fight. They dragged him downstairs and into their car, then sped off."

The story painted a clear picture of a well-planned and ruthless kidnapping. The kidnappers' boldness and determination suggested that they were professional criminals, and their interest in Hounsou indicated that he was more than just an innocent bystander caught up in their schemes. Boubou and Aya exchanged a look of concern, realizing how serious the situation was and the potential danger Hounsou was in.

"This is more complicated than we first thought. When gangsters start breaking into homes, it's a clear sign that things are getting serious," Boubou said.

Still riled up from the morning's events, the salt farmer strongly agreed. "You're right about it being serious," he said, pointing to the shotgun on the wall. "I've got this loaded now, ready for anyone else who dares to try something like this. I just wish I had it close by earlier today."

Trying to ease the farmer's worry, Boubou responded, "I don't think there's any more danger for you. They were after Hounsou, not you. It's unlikely they'll come back."

"They'd better not," Mr. Touma grumbled, his eyes fixed on the shotgun.

Aya turned to her brother, "We should head back to Zinguichou and tell Dad about what happened. There's nothing more we can do here right now."

Boubou nodded. "Yeah, let's go. Telling Dad through Grandma is the best move."

As they got ready to leave, Mr. Touma asked a question that made the Diouf siblings pause. "You said your last name is Diouf, right? Any relation to the late Malik Diouf?"

"He was our father," Boubou confirmed.

"The Detective? I heard he passed away," Mr. Touma said respectfully.

Aya nodded. "Yes, he did. But our grandmother keeps his memory alive."

"She's a clairvoyant," Boubou added.

Mrs. Touma's eyes lit up. "Ah, Grandma Diouf! I've heard about her. She's quite famous around here. Maybe we should see her after this. She might help make sense of things."

"That's a good idea," Mr. Touma agreed. "You kids go tell your dad through your grandmother. I'm sorry for your loss. If anyone could solve this mystery, it would've been him. It's terrible that those criminals are still out there."

After saying goodbye and wishing each other well, Boubou and Aya promised to return with any new information. Mr. Touma vowed to keep them informed of any news related to the kidnappers or Hounsou. With these promises, the brother and sister got on their bikes. They headed back towards Zinguichou, their minds busy with thoughts of the next steps in their unexpected adventure.

❖

As soon as they got home in Zinguichou, Boubou and Aya rushed to find their Grandma Diouf. She was enjoying a rare moment of relaxation, lost in a book. But the moment she saw the worried looks on her grandkids' faces, she put her reading aside, focusing on their apparent distress.

"Did Mr. Hounsou talk?" Grandma Diouf asked immediately, sensing from their expressions that something big had happened.

"We didn't even get to see him," Aya blurted out, frustrated and worried.

"Why? Did he leave?" Grandma Diouf asked, her eyebrows coming together in concern.

"He was kidnapped!" Boubou revealed, the seriousness of the situation clear in his tone.

"Kidnapped!" Grandma Diouf echoed in shock, her relaxing afternoon suddenly changed by this alarming news.

Boubou quickly shared the details, explaining how they found the mess at the Touma salt farm and learned about Hounsou being taken by four unknown men. Aya jumped in at times, adding to the story.

Grandma Diouf listened carefully. She understood how complex and dangerous the situation was. She now realized the seriousness of the events her grandkids had gotten involved in. Her worry for their safety was evident, but so was her decision to help them navigate this unexpected and risky mystery.

In response to the siblings' story, Grandma Diouf prepared for another clairvoyance session, seeking more guidance from their lost father. The room fell into a respectful silence as she focused, connecting with the spiritual world.

After a few suspenseful moments and a warm exchange of love from their mother and father, Grandma Diouf shared Mr. Diouf's message. "Your father believes that Hounsou was likely part of a criminal gang and either betrayed them or threatened to do so. They tried to kill him, and he managed to escape, but they assumed he was dead after the boat explosion."

"When they found out that you had rescued him, they took him from the salt farm house before he could share any information," Grandma Diouf continued.

Boubou, wanting more details, asked, "Does he think they're involved in smuggling?"

"Yes, he strongly suspects they are smugglers," Grandma Diouf confirmed. "And while you were out, I contacted the city police to share your story and the events of the past couple of days."

Aya, curious about another part of their investigation, asked, "Did you mention Scorpion to them?"

Grandma Diouf's smile was mysterious. "Not yet. I decided to hold back that information for now."

Aya thought about what that could mean. "It's starting to seem like Scorpion might actually be here in Zinguichou. He's the type who wouldn't hesitate to resort to kidnapping or even murder."

"Do the police have any suspicion that he's in this area?" Boubou asked.

"Chief Gaye brushed off the idea," she began. "In his typical style, he was quite certain that if any blood diamond smugglers were bold enough to operate in Zinguichou Bay, especially on a big scale, he'd definitely be the first to sniff them out. He scoffed at the idea, questioning how such activities could possibly go unnoticed under his watchful eye."

Aya, still wanting confirmation, urged, "Can you ask Dad again if he really thinks Scorpion is in Zinguichou?"

After connecting once more with the spiritual realm through the cowrie shells, Grandma Diouf shared the message she received, saying, "Your father believes it's likely. He once spoke with a special agent who indicated that the blood diamond smugglers they were tracking were active in this area. And Scorpion is known as a major player in blood diamond smuggling along the Atlantic coast."

Aya's excitement was evident. "Wow, imagine if we could catch him!"

Boubou, however, added a note of caution. "No one asked us to work on this case. I doubt Chief Gaye would allow us to get involved—it's quite dangerous."

"You mean officially?" Aya cut in, her eyes sparkling with excitement and determination.

"I'm not too keen on teaming up with the police, you know. Have you forgotten the whole Countess diamond mess at the Lighthouse? The police wouldn't believe us, and Abdou's father almost went to jail," Boubou reminded her, sounding skeptical.

Aya, always optimistic, jumped in, "But think about it, Boubou! If we actually caught this Scorpion guy, it'd be a huge deal for us."

Boubou raised an eyebrow. "Why's that?"

"The cash reward, obviously!" Aya replied with a hint of excitement.

Boubou's curiosity grew. "Is there really a reward out for this Scorpion character?"

At that moment, Grandma Diouf, who had been quietly listening, spoke up. "Indeed, there's a huge sum of $50,000 up for grabs for anyone who can bring in Scorpion. And considering your suspicions about him being in Zinguichou Bay, you kids might just have a shot at claiming that reward. You should tell the police about your theory and let them take it from there. It's way too dangerous for children."

Boubou's eyes lit up. "Please, Grandma, you know how our police handle things around here, don't you?"

"Yeah," Aya agreed enthusiastically. "We should just go for it!"

Despite Chief Gaye's typical skepticism, the next day, Boubou and Aya decided to stop by the police station to share their latest findings before diving deeper into their own investigation. With the recent boat explosion and now a kidnapping adding urgency to their quest, they figured that even the local police, usually dismissive of their efforts, might this time lend a friendly ear and take their story seriously. It was a strategic move to keep themselves out of trouble and perhaps gain some much-needed official support for their unfolding mystery. The Diouf siblings, armed with new clues and a growing sense of responsibility, hoped their visit would mark a turning point in getting the authorities on their side.

Expecting the usual scoffs from Chief Gaye and Detective Diallo about their recent adventure, the Diouf siblings were surprised to find the station unusually quiet without the Chief's presence. They soon discovered that Chief Gaye was exceptionally out on an investigation.

Detective Diallo, tall and skinny, fanned himself with his big hat. In a solemn voice and full of admiration for the absent Chief, he told them, "Chief Gaye left at dawn to investigate something at the Touma salt farm. He didn't say when he'd be back but went alone, so it's probably not a big deal. He'll likely return by lunchtime."

Detective Diallo's eagerness to seem efficient was evident as he unnecessarily scribbled in his notebook, puffing up his chest to appear more authoritative. Meanwhile, Constable Sarr, clearly relieved to be spared from his usual tedious tasks, wore a dismissive smirk as he eyed the Diouf siblings. His attitude towards them was marked by a condescending tone, clearly because of their young age.

The Chief's unexpected absence left Boubou and Aya puzzled. Chief Gaye's sudden interest in their story was out of character, especially without his usual fanfare. Boubou and Aya wondered what could have made him go on such a secret investigation alone, especially since he had said their story wasn't believable. With their minds full of questions, they headed off to school, the funny and clumsy way the police station operated still in their thoughts.

On their way, Boubou and Aya ran into Aminata Correa and Mariama Sambou, two girls who were close friends with the siblings. Aminata, with her brown eyes and curls flowing down her back, always caught Boubou's eye. He found her quite captivating, not just for her striking looks and hazel eyes but also for her elegant appearance and lively, energetic nature.

Mariama, Adama Sambou's sister, was a plump girl with short hair. Aya thought she was "all right, for a girl," a reluctant admission from someone who wasn't too fond of her classmates' typical girlish behaviors. Aya liked Mariama's tomboyish attitude, which was a refreshing change from what she saw as the overly girly attitudes common at school.

The siblings hadn't expected their friends to hear about their recent adventure at Kambossa's place last Saturday. It turned out that Adama had told his sister, Mariama, who then told Aminata, making sure the news spread among their circle.

Aminata greeted them with a teasing tone as they walked, "So, how are our brave ghost hunters this fine morning?"

Boubou replied with a casual smile, "We're doing just fine."

Aminata couldn't resist a playful jab, "Oh, what a courageous group you boys are! Running away from a supposedly empty house!"

"That house was definitely not empty," Aya quickly said, her voice full of conviction. "And what about Adama's stolen gas? You think that was just his imagination?"

Aminata chuckled, "Looks like someone played a perfect prank on you all. Just wait until you get to school. I bet whoever did it will be bragging about it to everyone."

Boubou shrugged off the comment casually, "We'll handle it. If Adama hadn't been there with us, I would've suspected him, actually. It seems like the kind of prank he'd pull."

Mariama said, "Well, he's got an alibi this time. He was with you guys. And judging by how he talked about it when he came home, I'd say he was just as spooked as the rest of you."

When they got to school, Boubou and Aya found out that their adventure at the cliffside house was already the talk of the campus. However, unlike what they expected, no one stepped forward to claim responsibility for setting up what they had first thought was a practical joke. Adama and the other boys shared details of their creepy experiences. Still, as lunchtime approached, the mystery remained unsolved, leaving everyone puzzled.

On their way home, Aya shared her growing suspicion, "I'm starting to think this wasn't just a prank. Trust me, if someone had set this up, they'd be rushing to brag about it by now."

Boubou, deep in thought, added, "It seemed too complicated to be just a joke. It's like someone intentionally started these ghost stories to keep people away from Kambossa's place."

"And who can blame them? With all the strange noises, walls falling down, and the stolen gas, it's no wonder people avoid going there. It seems like they've got a very active ghost on their hands," Aya thought out loud.

Then, a new idea hit them. Boubou turned to Aya, "Do you think… could this have something to do with the blood diamond smugglers?"

The brother and sister exchanged a meaningful look, the wheels turning in their heads.

"There's a thought!" Aya exclaimed. "We've come across two weird things in one day. Maybe they're somehow connected."

The idea that the cliff house could be a strategic hideout for smugglers, scaring away curious visitors with ghost stories, struck the siblings as a possible theory. "It might just be a coincidence, but it does make sense. A 'haunted' house is the perfect cover for illegal activities," Boubou added.

Aya, caught up in the excitement of their theory, exclaimed, "Wow, I hadn't thought of that! I wonder what Chief Gaye would think of this idea."

"Let's head back to the station. Chief Gaye might be there now. We can share our thoughts with him," Boubou suggested.

However, when they returned to the station at lunchtime and then again after school, the mystery only deepened. Chief Gaye was nowhere to be found. His unusual absence, with no word of where he was, started to make them feel worried. Detective Diallo's call to the

Touma salt farm revealed that Chief Gaye had not shown up for his expected visit, leaving the salt harvesters equally concerned.

The police station's usual routine was thrown off balance. Detective Diallo and Constable Sarr, though used to the Chief's sudden disappearances, usually for silly reasons like naps or snacks, couldn't help but feel a growing unease about this unexplained long absence. The situation seemed to be straying from the Chief's normal patterns, causing a wave of worry among the officers and the Diouf siblings alike.

❖

The following day, Boubou couldn't shake off a nagging feeling that something wasn't right. "I can't explain it," he said, "but something feels off."

Aya nodded in agreement. "I feel the same. Chief Gaye has never really followed up on our leads before. Detective Diallo mentioned he never leaves without telling someone where he's going. He's always been reliable in that way."

"We'll just have to wait and see what happens," Boubou said, trying to stay positive. "He's the Chief of Police, and he's pretty good at his job, even though he always reminds us of that fact. There's a good chance we're worrying over nothing, but I can't help feeling that something's wrong."

Grandma Diouf, however, wasn't as worried. She laughed and reassured them, "Oh, he'll show up at the station when we least expect it. You two are just eager to start working on the Scorpion case. Maybe that's what he's investigating right now. He might even come back with some valuable information."

Aya's remark about Chief Gaye was full of sarcasm. "Yeah, right. Imagine Chief Gaye going undercover alone, single-handedly saving the city from dangerous smugglers!" she laughed.

Boubou joined in, a bit cynically, "And he'd love to let us do all the Detective work while he takes all the credit, as usual."

Accepting the situation, the Diouf siblings focused on their school responsibilities, setting aside their Detective dreams for now. With vacation coming up and exams needing their attention, they had little time to think about Chief Gaye's mysterious absence.

❖

However, by Friday afternoon, the situation took an unexpected turn. When they got home from school, they found Grandma Diouf in the living room, her attention focused on a note. Her expression clearly indicated that the message was important.

"Come here, kids," Grandma Diouf called. "Look at this and tell me what you think. Detective Diallo just dropped it off." Her tone was severe, showing that the note was important in the ongoing mystery of Chief Gaye's disappearance.

Boubou took the note from his grandmother, his curiosity growing. "Is this from Chief Gaye?" he asked eagerly.

"It seems so," she replied.

The brother and sister looked closely at the note. The message, quickly scribbled in pencil on a piece of torn paper, seemed to be in Chief Gaye's handwriting, or at least as much as they could figure out. The note was short and to the point:

"I won't be at my office for several days. Don't worry. I'm undercover. Don't tell anyone. Diallo, you're in charge."

The Chief's signature didn't give any clues about where he was or when the message was written.

Looking up from the note, Boubou asked, "When did this arrive?"

Grandma Diouf replied, "Detective Diallo brought it over just a little while ago. He didn't say much, just that it was from Chief Gaye."

"When exactly did they find this note?" Boubou asked.

"It was found early today. Detective Diallo and Constable Sarr discovered it slipped under the main door of the police station when they arrived for their morning shift. They suspected something was wrong and came to me for clairvoyance insight. But I immediately thought of you two and thought you could lend a hand with it," Grandma replied.

Putting together the timeline in his mind, Boubou nodded thoughtfully. "So, it was dropped off sometime during the night or early morning. That's interesting. Imagine that, Detective Diallo and Constable Sarr finding this note."

"They must've been like lost puppies without Chief Gaye. And now they come to us for help? That's hilarious!" Aya laughed.

Boubou chuckled at the image Aya painted. "I can see it now—Detective Diallo, walking around the station with that 'I'm in charge' look, but secretly panicking at the smallest hint of responsibility."

Aya, with a smirk, picked up the note again. "And this whole undercover thing with Chief Gaye, it's so funny," she added. "Since when has he done anything without making a big deal about it? He's the kind of guy who'd call a press conference to announce he's going undercover, not sneak away quietly."

Their laughter filled the room as they pictured the crazy scene at the police station. The thought of Detective Diallo, with his sincere yet often clumsy attempts at holding authority, taking the lead was enough to amuse them despite the seriousness of Chief Gaye's mysterious absence.

Grandma Diouf was clearly worried. "If he didn't write it, then who did?" she asked more seriously.

Regaining his composure, Boubou shook his head, brushing off the laughter. "You're right, Grandma. As funny as this whole situation is, we need to figure out what's really going on. If this note isn't from Chief Gaye, then where is he? And why would someone want us to think he's undercover?"

Aya nodded, her expression turning thoughtful. "Yeah, leaving a mysterious note under the door? That doesn't make sense. Chief Gaye would have made sure everyone knew about his 'heroic' departure."

"We can't let ourselves get distracted. There's clearly more to this than just a note and Detective Diallo playing Chief," said Boubou. "Obviously, someone's trying to pass this note off as the Chief's."

"Okay, let's put on our thinking caps," Boubou suggested with a serious tone. "Chief Gaye has a long list of enemies. Think about it—some folks are mad because their criminal relatives got caught by him, and then there are the ones he put away who've done their time and are now out of jail. If something shady is going on, that note might just be a trick to throw the cops off the trail and slow down any search efforts."

"Something shady?" Grandma's voice rose in surprise and worry. "You don't really believe that something bad has happened to Chief Gaye, do you?" she asked, her face reflecting her growing concern.

"The thing is, the Chief just disappearing out of nowhere like this? It's just not like him," Boubou thought out loud. "Why else would someone send a note like that to the station if not to stop them from looking for him?"

Aya stood up, her determination clear. "Whether he wrote that note or someone else did, we're going to find him," she declared confidently. "He didn't tell us not to worry. He didn't say we shouldn't look for him. If he did write it, we're not exactly disobeying him, right? And imagine us rescuing the Chief of Police. That would be awesome!"

"You've got a point!" Boubou agreed, his voice filled with excitement. "Our vacation starts next week. We'll have all the time in the world to track him down."

"Maybe wait until then," Grandma Diouf suggested cautiously. "He might be back before that." Yet, as she looked at the note once more, examining the signature and sensing something off about the Chief's unusual departure, her fear that Chief Gaye might really be in danger grew stronger.

✳ ✳ ✳

CHAPTER NINE

Tracing The Chief's Steps

Chief Gaye was still missing when summer vacation started. At first, his wife stayed calm. Being married to a police officer, she knew the risks that came with his job. She had learned not to worry too much about things she couldn't control. It was an unspoken rule to never question the dangers he faced.

But this time was different. Chief Gaye had never disappeared for so long without a word. It wasn't like him at all. He was known for being proud and caring a lot about his reputation. His job often required him to leave suddenly on missions, sometimes with Detective Diallo. These trips could last for days, and while the Chief usually kept his location a secret for safety reasons, he always sent a comforting message to his wife, keeping in touch even when he couldn't say where he was.

Apart from one weird note, there had been no word from him. Since he left the police station that morning after the kidnapping at the Touma salt farm, Chief Gaye had vanished as if the earth had swallowed him whole. The silence was strange, and the mystery of his disappearance grew bigger each day.

Detective Diallo and Constable Sarr searched all over Zinguichou but kept hitting dead ends. No one remembered seeing Chief Gaye on the day he vanished. At the train station, they found out that the Chief hadn't bought a ticket, not that day or the days after. The ticket agent said it was possible the Chief had gotten on a train and paid on board, but he didn't think it was likely. They asked similar questions at the steamboat office, but Chief Gaye hadn't been seen there either.

Local shopkeepers and street vendors, who knew the Chief well, also hadn't seen him that morning. It was odd since the Chief was known for leaving his house early and was a familiar face in the city. Determined to find answers, the siblings asked everyone who might have seen him: schoolmates, early-rising farmers, and regular commuters. But the more they investigated, the deeper the mystery of Chief Gaye's disappearance became, leaving them with more questions than answers.

Abdou Ngom, whom his friends called Doudou, was super curious about Chief Gaye's disappearance. Doudou's family had been caught up in a local scandal about some missing diamonds, something people in Zinguichou called "The Lighthouse Mystery." During that tough time, the Diouf family had been there for the Ngoms, and Doudou's family was really grateful for their support.

"Hey, guys, I actually saw the Chief on the street not too long ago," Abdou said, excitement in his voice. "He even waved at me."

Boubou, always quick to catch on, asked eagerly, "When did that happen?"

"It was just a day or two before he went missing," Doudou replied. You could see on his face how much he wanted to help. "Man, I really wish I could do more to help you guys find him!"

Aya, practical as always, encouraged him, "Well, Doudou, just keep your eyes open, and if you notice anything, no matter how small, let us know, okay?"

Abdou nodded excitedly, ready to help out however he could.

Not long after talking with Abdou Ngom, the siblings ran into a group of their friends, including the lovely Aminata Correa. Aminata, her long braids swaying gently as she approached, greeted them with a worried look. "Hey, Boubou, Aya," she called out, her voice tinged with concern.

"Hi, Aminata," Boubou replied, his voice softening and a broad smile spreading across his face. His heart skipped a beat, and he stood a little taller, trying to impress her despite the tension in the air. "What's up?"

Aminata glanced around, lowering her voice as if to keep their conversation private. "I heard about Chief Gaye. It's all anyone can talk about. I saw him too, a few days ago, early in the morning."

"Really?" Aya asked, her eyes widening. "What did he say to you?"

Aminata's face brightened with a hint of amusement as she recalled the encounter. "Well, you won't believe this, but he actually let something slip about a 'secret mission' he was on. He was acting all mysterious and kept looking around like he was in a spy movie," she said, rolling her eyes and chuckling.

Boubou raised an eyebrow. "Chief Gaye? On a secret mission?"

"Yeah," Aminata said, giggling. "He pulled me aside and whispered, 'Aminata, you mustn't tell anyone, but I'm on a top-secret mission.'"

"Sounds totally like our Chief!" Aya laughed.

"And then," Aminata continued, struggling to keep a straight face, "he puffed out his chest and said, 'I've been chosen for a critical task. Very hush-hush. Only for the bravest and smartest, you know.'"

Aya snickered. "Did he actually say 'hush-hush'?"

Aminata nodded, her eyes rolling. "He did! And he looked so proud of himself. I think he couldn't help but boast a little. He told me he was tracking down a notorious smuggler. Something about a salt farm. He said it was a job only he could handle."

"Oh, this is too good," Aya chuckled. "So he did take our story seriously!"

Aminata shook her head, still smiling. "Then, he got all serious and said, 'That's all I can tell you, young lady. But remember, not a word to anyone!' And then he winked and walked away, trying to look all cool."

Despite the urgency of the situation, the siblings couldn't help but smile, the tension easing slightly with the amusing image of Chief Gaye trying to play the role of a secret agent.

After talking it over, Boubou realized that Aminata had bumped into the Chief several days before he vanished. The information, though interesting, was dated and not very useful. Still, there was a chance that his so-called secret mission could be connected to his disappearance.

Aminata looked extremely worried as she said, "Oh, I'm so sorry this happened." Boubou and Aya nodded, feeling the same way. You could see the concern on their faces.

Clearly, the Chief's disappearance had left everyone in their tight-knit community feeling uneasy.

"Don't worry, Aminata," Boubou said, his tone becoming serious again. "We'll figure this out."

"Yeah," Aya agreed, her face determined. "We'll bring him back."

Aminata managed a small, hopeful smile. "Thanks, Boubou. I know you will. Just…be careful, okay? Something about this feels off."

The group fell into a thoughtful silence, the weight of the Chief's disappearance pressing down on them. They knew they had to act, but the uncertainty of the situation left a heavy feeling in the air.

"Let's meet up later," Boubou suggested, his voice firm. Then he turned to Aya: "We need a plan."

❖

The Diouf siblings were determined to search everywhere for clues. From their encounter with Aminata, they figured Chief Gaye had taken their story seriously and might have gone to check out the

Touma salt farm. Convinced this might be the case, they headed there, hoping to find some hint of where he might be.

When they arrived, they found Mr. Touma working in the salt ponds. Mrs. Touma greeted them at the gate with a warm smile.

"Hello, Boubou, Aya. What brings you here today?" Mrs. Touma asked, wiping her hands on her apron.

"We're looking for any clues about Chief Gaye's disappearance," Boubou said. "We think he might have come here."

Mrs. Touma's expression turned serious. "Oh dear, I haven't seen him. Let's ask my husband."

They followed Mrs. Touma to the salt ponds, where Mr. Touma was busy working. He looked up, surprised to see the children.

"Mr. Touma, have you seen Chief Gaye recently?" Aya asked, her voice hopeful.

"No one has visited the farm since that crazy Sunday when the kidnapping happened," Mr. Touma replied, shaking his head.

"They've left us alone, thank goodness!" Mrs. Touma added, sounding relieved. "Since those troublemakers left, no one's been near the house."

"We know Chief Gaye very well. He's hard to miss, if you catch my drift. We definitely would have noticed if he had been around," Mr. Touma replied.

Mrs. Touma nodded in agreement. "He's right. Catching up with all the work, especially after tending to that Hounsou character, we would have noticed anyone unusual. Taking care of him has set us back quite a bit."

Boubou sighed, looking at Aya. "This news only makes the mystery of the Chief's disappearance even more puzzling."

"Do you think he might have gone somewhere else after checking the farm?" Aya asked, her brow furrowed in thought.

"It's possible," Boubou replied. "But we have no other leads right now."

Mrs. Touma placed a comforting hand on Aya's shoulder. "I'm sure you'll find him. Keep looking, and don't lose hope."

"Thank you, Mrs. Touma," Aya said, managing a small smile. "We won't give up."

As they left the farm, Boubou and Aya exchanged worried glances, wondering what they should do next to solve this deepening mystery.

❖

Returning to Zinguichou, the brother and sister felt confused and disappointed. The failed search at the Touma salt farm left them wondering about Chief Gaye's whereabouts. They couldn't imagine where else he could be if not there.

"Something has happened to him; I'm sure of it," Boubou said, his voice filled with concern. "It isn't like Chief Gaye to be away this long without sending a message to his wife, Diallo, and Sarr."

Aya thought, "Maybe he did write that note."

But Boubou wasn't convinced. "He would have explained more in the note, you know? And he would have left some kind of secret clue to help us find him if he needed help."

As the siblings' efforts to find their local Chief of Police became the talk of Zinguichou, their search drew unexpected attention. One evening, a thick-set, broad-shouldered man showed up at the Diouf house, looking for the siblings. Grandma Diouf, always the gracious host, invited him in. He stood in the hall, nervously twisting his cap between his hands.

When Boubou and Aya came out, the stranger introduced himself. "I'm Demba Akoum," he said, with the unhurried manner of someone used to life's slower pace. Then, he started to unfold his story. "I'm a truck driver," he began again, stressing his job as if it were crucial to his story. "I came over because I heard you were looking for the Chief of Police."

"Have you seen him? Do you know where he is?" Boubou asked, his eagerness clear.

Demba shuffled his feet slightly, his gaze shifting to the floor. "Well, yes and no, I guess," he said thoughtfully. "I did see the Chief a few days ago, but as to where he is now, I couldn't say. I really don't know." Demba spoke slowly and carefully, giving weight to even the most obvious statements as though they were deep revelations.

"So, where did you see him?" Boubou pressed.

"I'm a truck driver," Demba repeated, as though this fact provided some critical context.

"Yes, you mentioned that," Boubou said, impatience creeping into his voice. "But where exactly did you see the Chief?"

Demba was not one to be rushed. He had a story to share and intended to tell it in his own methodical, unhurried way. "I usually drive around Zinguichou, but occasionally, they send me out to some of the surrounding villages. That's how I ended up out there that morning."

"Out where?" Boubou asked, trying to keep the conversation focused.

"I'm getting to that," Demba said, a hint of storytelling flair in his voice. "I can't remember the exact day, but it was about a week after the previous Monday. It had to be just after Sunday because that's when I came home for dinner, and my wife was doing laundry. Dinner was late, and I had to eat it on the back steps since the kitchen was all in a mess. You know how crazy wash day can be."

Demba looked at them, almost expecting a nod of understanding or sympathy. However, the Diouf siblings, driven by their search for information, were growing impatient with his roundabout storytelling.

"But how does this relate to the Chief?" Aya asked, her voice laced with urgency.

"I'm getting there," Demba reassured them. "Just bear with me. Like I said, I think it was a Monday because that's the only day my wife does the laundry. I mean, she washes clothes only on Mondays. She, of course, washes herself every day. So, it was definitely a Monday."

"That was the same day Chief Gaye disappeared," Boubou added, hoping to guide Demba's story toward the Chief's last known movements.

Demba's eyes widened in surprise. "Really? Well, now, that's something. Yes, I saw him that day."

"Where did you see him?" the siblings asked eagerly.

Taking his time, Demba continued, "I'm getting to that part. As I was saying, it was a Monday. I went down to the garage, and my boss tells me, 'Demba, I need you to take a truckload of poultry seed sacks down the shore road.' So, I replied, 'Well, boss, that's what I'm here for.' He mentioned that these sacks of seeds needed to be delivered to a farmhouse near the cliff. So, we loaded up the truck, I filled her up with gas, and off I went. It must have been around nine in the morning, I guess."

"And you drove down the shore road?" Boubou asked to confirm.

"Exactly. It was a really nice morning for a drive," Demba recounted. "I drove past the Lighthouse—you know, Countess Mbaye's place, the one where you two kids found those diamonds. I was just driving along, whistling and feeling carefree, when I realized I was approaching that haunted house on the cliff. The place where the old fisherman was killed, you know?"

"Kambossa's place!" Boubou and Aya said simultaneously, recognizing the reference to the infamous local landmark.

"Yeah, that's the one," Demba confirmed. "So, I was driving past there and wasn't going slow, mind you. Everyone says that place is haunted, and I wasn't about to take any chances with ghosts or anything like that. I was driving at a good speed when suddenly, I saw a man walking along the road."

"Did he head down the path leading to Kambossa's place?" asked Boubou.

"I can't say for sure if he went down to Kambossa's place," Demba replied, scratching his head thoughtfully. "He hadn't quite reached the lane when I last saw him. And on my way back, I didn't see him, so I really don't know where he might've gone. To be honest, I didn't think much more about it until this morning. Some of us were hanging around the garage, chatting, and one guy mentioned that you kids had been searching all over the city for the Chief and couldn't find him. That got me thinking, 'Demba, maybe you've got something to tell them that they don't know.' So, I decided to come up and share what I saw."

"We really appreciate that," Boubou responded gratefully. "You've given us some important clues. We weren't sure if the Chief had left the city. Now, we have a new direction to explore."

Looking a bit concerned, Demba then asked, "You don't think there's any chance of him snooping around that Kambossa place, do you? From what everyone says, it's a place best avoided. They say it's haunted, you know." His tone conveyed a mix of curiosity and a hint of superstition.

"That wouldn't scare him; he's pretty brave," Aya reassured, though her confidence didn't quite match her words.

Boubou said with gratitude, "But it's perfect you told us about seeing him. Now we have a clearer idea of where to start looking."

Demba Akoum nodded, satisfied that he could be of help. "Glad to have been of help. I guess I'll be heading off now," he said, adjusting his cap. "Here's hoping the Chief turns up safe and sound."

The Diouf siblings expressed their thanks warmly as Akoum walked off, his hands tucked in his pockets.

Soon after, Grandma Diouf appeared in the hallway, her forehead wrinkled with concern. "Any news?" she asked anxiously.

Boubou responded with a hint of optimism, "We've got a clue now. That man, Akoum, said he saw Chief Gaye on the shore road the morning he disappeared."

"Where exactly did you see him?" Grandma Diouf asked for details.

"Near that old Kambossa place," Boubou explained.

"The haunted house on the cliff?" Grandma's voice carried a mix of disbelief and concern.

Boubou simply nodded to confirm.

Grandma Diouf's expression became even more severe. "It's hard to believe he would go there and then just vanish," she thought out loud.

Deep in thought, Boubou added, "Yeah, I can't figure out why he'd head to the house on the cliff. It doesn't make sense."

Suddenly, Aya's face lit up with realization. "Oh! Now I remember something important!" she exclaimed. "I completely forgot to tell you about it earlier. It was almost like a dream or a nightmare. But now, with all this talk about Kambossa's place, it's come back to me."

Intrigued, Boubou leaned in closer. "What was it?"

"When we were digging into the whole Scorpion case, the blood diamond smugglers, I had this crazy vivid dream. Dad was there with me," Aya began.

Boubou, puzzled, asked, "What do you mean, 'Dad was there?'"

Aya took a deep breath, ready to share something deeply personal. "You know, sometimes I feel this strange, psychic connection with Dad. It's like images or messages just pop into my mind out of nowhere. They're intense and sometimes scary, but they always feel warm and caring. After that dream about Scorpion, I woke up feeling restless. So, I played with my cowrie shells in bed, and it was like Dad was speaking to me, just like he does with Grandma."

Grandma Diouf's smile held a touch of wisdom and understanding. She had always been aware of the unique gift Aya possessed, a gift of clairvoyance similar to her own, but she had chosen to stay silent. Grandma believed in the natural unfolding of such abilities and never wanted to impose or rush Aya into realizing her potential. She knew Aya would come to understand and embrace her gift in her own time, just as she had now begun to do.

"And what did Dad say to you?" Boubou asked, his voice tinged with skepticism and intrigue.

Aya's eyes widened as she recalled the revelation. "He seemed to be hinting that Scorpion was somehow related to Kambossa, the old miser who lived in that haunted house."

"Related to him?" Boubou echoed, surprised by this unexpected connection.

"He was either a cousin or a nephew, something like that. One of the government agents mentioned it to Dad one day," Aya continued. "Dad figured that Kambossa must have had a visit from Scorpion at some point, and it was then that Scorpion came up with the idea to use Zinguichou Bay for his smuggling."

"Whew!" Grandma Diouf exclaimed, her eyes widening with realization. "Now things are starting to make sense. Chief Gaye must have gone to Kambossa's house to look into this."

Aya's frustration was evident. "I can't believe I overlooked this," she lamented. "Why didn't we think to search there sooner? I always had this nagging feeling about a link between the strange things that happened at Kambossa's place when we visited and the case of Hounsou, who we rescued. Then, that night, learning from Dad about Scorpion's connection to Kambossa, it all seemed to click. It was as clear as daylight. But when I woke up, it all became blurry, and I dismissed it as just a weird dream." Her regret was clear, but her voice also had a new resolve.

"Don't be too hard on yourself, dear. It's not your fault," Grandma Diouf reassured Aya gently. "But what could have possibly happened to Chief Gaye?" she wondered aloud, her concern evident.

"We should head up to Kambossa's place and see for ourselves," Boubou declared with determination.

However, Grandma Diouf raised a cautionary hand. Her expression was serious, her lips set in a firm line. "Promise me, you two won't go there alone."

"Why not, Grandma? We can handle ourselves," Boubou protested.

"If something has happened to Chief Gaye, I don't want you two facing the same danger," Grandma insisted, her voice tinged with worry.

"But we have to go there to search the place thoroughly," Aya argued.

"Then take some of your friends with you," Grandma suggested. "It'll be safer that way."

Aya nodded in agreement. "That's a good idea. We'll gather a bunch of the guys and head there first thing in the morning. We'll search through that place carefully this time."

Satisfied with this plan, Grandma Diouf gave her consent. Boubou and Aya immediately set out to gather their friends for the expedition. Although a few hesitated, especially when they heard the destination was the infamous haunted house, most were intrigued and willing. By nightfall, everything was arranged for their journey the next day.

CHAPTER TEN

The Unexpected Occupants

THE FOLLOWING DAY, THE SEARCH PARTY WAS READY TO GO. Amath and Bouma were still freaked out by the spooky stuff that happened during their first trip to Kambossa's house, so they decided to sit this one out. But Adama and Bacary, along with their good friends from Zinguichou Middle School, Mouhamed, and Pierre Leroy, showed up. Adama even brought his cool sidecar motorcycle, which made the whole thing feel like an adventure. The rest of the group had their shiny new bikes, and they all looked like a team of superheroes ready to save the day.

Before they left, Boubou gathered everyone together to explain the plan. "We think Chief Gaye was last seen around Kambossa's place," he said, his face serious. "He probably went there to check out the house. But he never came back, and nobody's seen him since. We have to consider the possibility that something bad might've happened." His words made everyone feel how important their mission was.

"If there's any clue about where he is near Kambossa's house, we'll find it for sure," Adama said confidently. "And this time, no ghost, no matter how scary, will make us run away."

Mouhamed nodded, adjusting his hat. "We've got each other's backs. If something goes down, we stick together."

"Absolutely," Pierre agreed. "And hey, if we do run into any ghosts, we can always scare them away with Amath's ghost dogs."

Amath rolled his eyes with frustration. "Hilarious, Pierre. Let's see you laugh when my ghost dogs bite your butt."

Boubou chimed in, "Ok. Let's just chill, guys. Everyone ready?"

"Ready!" the group responded in unison, their determination clear.

Aya smiled at Boubou, "Let's go find Chief Gaye and solve this mystery. We've got this."

Boubou nodded, his expression firm. "Alright, team. Let's move out!"

With that, the group set off towards Kambossa's house, their hearts filled with excitement and determination, ready to face whatever lay ahead.

The bikes zoomed out of Zinguichou, flying by the Lighthouse and racing down the road along the beach. Nobody was laughing or joking around. They all knew this wasn't just a fun bike ride; it was a serious mission, and everyone understood its importance.

As they rode, Boubou turned to Aya. "You think we'll find anything today?" he asked, keeping his voice low but hopeful.

Aya nodded. "I'm sure we will. We just have to stay sharp and stick together."

Pierre, riding up beside them, chimed in. "Hey, I know you two can handle this."

Mouhamed, a bit quieter than the others, spoke up. "I just hope Chief Gaye is okay. It's weird not knowing what happened to him."

"You mean Mr. 'Top Secret Mission' himself?" chuckled Bacary. "I can just imagine him trying to impress some smuggler with his 'special detective skills.'"

Adama grinned. "Yeah, and then tripping over his own feet two seconds later. Classic Chief Gaye."

"Probably got himself stuck in a cupboard and can't find his way out," Aya joked.

As they continued riding, the group fell into a comfortable rhythm, the sound of their bike tires humming along the road. The beach stretched out beside them, the waves crashing softly against the shore.

"Remember, if anyone sees anything strange, shout out," Boubou reminded them. "We can't afford to miss anything."

Aya glanced at Boubou, her eyes determined. "We'll find him, Boubou. I know we will."

Boubou and Aya trusted their friends completely. They weren't totally sure how Bacary and Mouhamed would handle being scared. Still, they had no worries about Adama and Pierre. Everyone at school knew those two were brave—sometimes even a little reckless. They had already shown how tough and clever they could be on that unforgettable night when the gang tricked the police during the Lighthouse mystery. With such a fantastic team, the siblings felt supported and ready as they pedaled towards whatever awaited them at Kambossa's house.

As they continued, the group rode past the Touma farm, tucked away cozily in the trees. Pretty soon, the dark, scary shape of the gloomy cliff appeared, rising steeply from Zinguichou Bay. Perched on top of this cliff was the big, rambling stone house where the stingy old Kambossa used to live before he died suddenly.

"It sure looks lonely, doesn't it?" Mouhamed said, trying to sound casual as he rode safely next to Boubou's bike.

"It's the perfect place for something creepy to happen. Back when Kambossa lived there, I bet he didn't get more than two or three visitors a year," Boubou replied.

Curious, Pierre asked, "How did he get food and stuff?"

"Well, when Kambossa was still fishing, he used to buy his groceries at the local market like everyone else. He ate a lot of fish, of course. But after he got rich, he hired old Lassana Yade. In this rickety old buggy, he'd drive into the city about once a week."

"With his horse that looked like it came straight out of Noah's Ark," Aya added with a small smile. "The poor thing always seemed like it was starving."

Their talk made the place seem even more exciting and mysterious as they got closer, getting ready for whatever they might find at the old Kambossa house.

"Kambossa must have been a little crazy, living all alone up there," Bacary said thoughtfully. "The man worked hard at sea and knew how to make good money from fishing. No one could beat him when it came to selling fish and lobster."

As they approached, Mouhamed stared hard at the old gray house, seeing more details with each pedal push. But before they reached the lane leading to the house, Boubou suddenly stopped his bike and signaled for the others to stop, too.

"What's up?" Adama asked, confused.

"We should sneak up on the place quietly," Boubou suggested. "If someone's there, they'll hear Adama's motorcycle or see our bikes. Let's hide them here under the trees and walk the rest of the way."

Everyone nodded in agreement. They quickly hid their bikes and the motorcycle in a secret spot among the trees, getting ready to tiptoe towards the mysterious house on foot, keeping their eyes and ears open for any sign of Chief Gaye or unexpected visitors.

The bikes were now hidden carefully in a clump of bushes by the road as the six teens headed toward the lane leading to the mysterious house.

"We should split up here," Boubou suggested, sounding like he was in charge. "Let's break into two groups. Three of us will take one side of the lane, and the other three will take the opposite side. Stay as hidden as possible in the bushes, and when we're close to the house, we'll stop and watch. I'll whistle when it's time to come out and go up to the house."

"That sounds like a good plan," Aya agreed. "Pierre, Bacary, and I will take the left side of the road."

"Okay. Adama, Mouhamed, and I will take the right side. Remember, stay out of sight of the house as much as possible," Boubou instructed.

The group then split up as planned, each trio sneaking their way through the thick underbrush lining their sides of the lane. The only signs of their movement were the occasional sounds of branches snapping and leaves rustling under their feet.

As Boubou led his group through the dense bushes, he carefully moved, knowing they needed to be quiet. The undergrowth was thicker and harder to get through than he had expected, slowing them down. Every step was careful and deliberate as they tried to get close to the house without making too much noise. After about ten minutes of sneaking, Boubou raised his hand, signaling the others to stop.

Peeking through the thicket, he got his first look at the house. They kept inching forward until they reached the edge of the bushes. There, they crouched down low, using the leaves as cover, their eyes glued to the gloomy old stone building across the clearing.

But something immediately struck Boubou as weird, making him look surprised. Kambossa's house, which everyone thought was abandoned and sad, was showing clear signs that someone was living there.

The change in Kambossa's house was shocking. Where once wild weeds had taken over the yard, they were now cleared away, showing neatly cut grass. The broken-down fence, which had been a sign of neglect, was now fixed and standing straight. The gate, which used to dangle on just one hinge, was now properly attached. The pathway had also been cleaned up, with the overgrown grass trimmed neatly.

This change wasn't just on the outside. Once boarded up with no glass, the house's windows now shined with new panes. The front door, which had looked old and neglected, was repaired, and the steps leading up to it had been fixed. A clear sign that someone lived there was the thin wisp of smoke curling up from the kitchen chimney.

"There must be someone living here," Adama whispered, his voice barely loud enough to hear.

Boubou, equally surprised, tried to make sense of the situation. It was news to him that anyone had moved into the famously haunted house. Given the house's creepy reputation, any new people moving in would have definitely stirred up gossip in Zinguichou. Yet, there had been no whispers, no rumors.

The gang stayed huddled at the edge of the bushes, their eyes fixed on the house, noticing every detail. Seeing a woman come out to hang clothes on a line in the backyard only made them more confused. She moved like someone at home, doing normal, everyday things.

Then another man came out. He walked across the yard with purposeful steps, heading straight for the shed where they had once parked their bikes during the storm. Once there, he started working on a big car and focused on his task. The scene in front of them was the total opposite of what they expected. They had been ready for the creepy, deserted feel that had marked their last visit. Instead, they found themselves watching ordinary, even peaceful, household activities. It was a situation that none of them could understand.

Realizing that staying hidden wasn't helping anymore, Boubou whispered firmly, "No point hiding. Let's regroup and ask them directly."

He let out a low whistle, signaling the others, and then stepped out from the shelter of the bushes into the lane. His friends quickly followed. Shortly after, Aya and the rest of the group, who had been on the other side, joined them.

The gang was clearly puzzled by the dramatic change in Kambossa's place.

Aya shook her head in disbelief. "This is beyond weird," she said. "It seems like some new family has moved in, but it's so strange that nobody in Zinguichou has mentioned it. If someone had the guts to live in the 'haunted' Kambossa place, it would definitely be the talk of the town."

Boubou, determined, added, "We need answers. Let's go up and talk to them."

With a shared sense of purpose, the six teenagers confidently left the cover of the lane and walked across the yard toward the house. Their approach didn't go unnoticed. The man working on the car in the shed spotted them first. He paused, setting down his wrench, and looked at them with surprise and annoyance. The woman, busy with the laundry, heard them coming and turned to face them, putting her hands on her hips. She looked stern and unwelcoming, her clothes messy, leaving the group with a not-so-great first impression.

"What do you want?" the man called out as he stepped out of the shed, his tone rude and guarded. The group stopped, ready to confront the unexpected inhabitants of Kambossa's house, feeling a bit nervous.

The man confronting them was short and skinny, with short hair and clearly needing a shave. His dark skin stood out against narrow eyes under rough, black eyebrows. His approach was blunt and far from friendly, showing his annoyance at their unexpected arrival.

At the same time, another man came out of the house, standing imposingly on the steps. Stout and grey-bearded, with a thick mustache, he gave off an air of challenge as he glared at the group in his shirt sleeves.

"Yeah, what's the big idea?" he demanded, echoing his companion's unfriendly tone.

Boubou, staying calm, took the lead in responding. "We didn't know anyone was living here," he said, subtly moving closer to the kitchen door to try and catch a glimpse inside.

"Well, there is," the grey-bearded man retorted. "We're living here now, and I don't see how that's any of your business. Why are you snooping around?"

"We aren't snooping," Boubou replied calmly. "We're looking for a man who has disappeared from Zinguichou."

The woman merely grunted in response to their explanation, clearly skeptical.

The grey-bearded man, still standing firmly on the steps, questioned further. "What makes you think he might be here?"

Boubou answered, "He was last seen in this neighborhood."

"What's his name?" the man continued.

"Gaye," Boubou replied.

"And what does he look like?" the man pressed.

"Short, chubby, and he was wearing his police uniform and cap," Boubou described.

"Yeah, he's the Chief of police," Aya added, emphasizing their search's importance.

"Ain't been no copper around here since we moved in," the grey-bearded man responded bluntly.

"No, we haven't seen him," the woman interjected sharply. "You kids better go look somewhere else."

Realizing that more questions would be pointless with the unwelcoming trio, the group reluctantly got ready to leave. However, Boubou, who had managed to get close to the open door during the talk, caught a glimpse of something inside. It was a police cap hanging clearly on a peg.

✳ ✳ ✳

CHAPTER ELEVEN

In Pursuit Of Answers

Boubou's mind raced, desperate to find out the truth. The police cap in front of him looked way too familiar. It looked just like the one Chief Gaye wore that morning at the station. "Could it really be the same one?" Boubou wondered. Everyone knew these caps were part of the police uniform. Still, he needed a closer look; there was always a chance it could be a similar-looking army cap. He couldn't risk jumping to conclusions without being totally sure.

Feeling a sudden need to know the truth, Boubou blurted out, "I'm super thirsty. Can I grab a drink of water?"

Grayhead and the woman glanced at each other hesitantly. Obviously, they wanted Boubou and his friends to leave, but saying no to such a simple request would be rude. Unwillingly, they agreed, hiding their impatience with a fake smile.

"Kitchen's this way," Grayhead muttered, sounding really reluctant. Boubou couldn't have asked for a better chance. He followed Grayhead into Kambossa's kitchen, his eyes darting around, taking in every detail. Grayhead pointed towards the sink, where a clean glass sat waiting in the dish rack.

"Just help yourself," Grayhead said, barely hiding his impatience.

As Boubou moved towards the sink, he passed by the hanging cap. A quick, sneaky glance was all he needed. His suspicions were correct—it was definitely Chief's cap. But then, something caught his eye, making him jolt. For a split second, he almost froze, but he quickly got his cool back and kept going to the tap. This was more serious than he had thought.

The cap had bloodstains on it.

The three large, reddish stains on the lower edge of the cap could only be one thing—blood. Boubou's heart raced as he realized this alarming discovery. Trying to act normal, he filled the glass with water and took a long, thoughtful sip. He could feel Greybeard's eyes staring at him, watching his every move.

"Thanks," Boubou said casually, glancing once more where the cap had been. It was gone. Greybeard must have quickly removed it while Boubou was distracted. Keeping his cool, Boubou left the kitchen and rejoined his friends outside.

"It's time to head out," he announced, trying to sound casual.

"About time," the woman snapped, clearly annoyed. "No strangers here, you know."

"We're sorry to have bothered you," Aya chimed in politely. "Goodbye."

Greybeard's response was a gruff grunt. The woman and the other man stayed silent as the group left, heading back to the lane. They walked quietly, lost in thought, the weight of the discovery hanging heavy in the air.

Once they were at a safe distance from the house and out of earshot, Boubou turned to his friends, ready to share what he had found.

"Do you guys get why I wanted to go into the kitchen?" Boubou asked, his eyes scanning the faces of his friends.

"Why?" they asked together, their curiosity sparked. Aya added, "You seemed to have a plan when you asked for that drink. What's up?"

Boubou paused for effect, "Chief Gaye's cap was just hanging there on a peg!"

Their reactions were instant and intense. Pierre let out a low whistle, clearly shocked. "So he was here! They've been lying to us!"

"But are you sure it was his cap?" Aya questioned.

"Absolutely sure. I'd know that cap anywhere. And that's not all," Boubou said, his voice dropping. "It had bloodstains on it."

"Bloodstains!" their voices echoed with surprise and worry.

Boubou simply nodded, confirming the grim discovery. They all exchanged looks, a silent understanding passing between them. The seriousness of what they'd stumbled upon was still on their minds.

"This is super serious," Aya declared. "There's no way we're just going to ignore this."

"Yeah, we can't just walk away from this," Adama said, determination in his tone. "We should head back there."

Boubou nodded, explaining his earlier caution, "I was about to confront them then and there, but I wanted you guys in the loop first. You needed to know what's going on."

Aya's voice trailed off, "He might have been..." She couldn't finish the sentence.

"He might have been murdered," Boubou said, not shying away from the grim possibility. "And we're going to get to the bottom of it."

"So, what's the plan?" Pierre asked, looking around at the group.

"We go back, tell them we saw the cap, and ask them straight up how it got there," Boubou suggested. "They already don't like us much, so we don't need to beat around the bush."

After a quick group discussion, they all agreed. The situation was too critical to ignore, and the creepy nature of the people at Kambossa's house, coupled with the discovery of Chief Gaye's cap, was a clue they couldn't overlook.

Boubou added, "He hid the cap the moment I turned away. That's a dead giveaway something's off."

"That alone proves we're onto something," Adama stated. "Let's confront them now."

"No time to waste. Let's get moving," Aya said, stepping forward, ready to lead the way back. The group, united in their purpose, set off, determined to uncover the truth.

❖

As the group retraced their steps down the lane, a sense of determination hung in the air. Approaching the house, they spotted the two men and the woman deep in conversation by the shed. They were so focused on their talk that they didn't notice the kids until they were almost upon them. The woman, spotting the group, alerted Greybeard with a nudge.

"What do you want now?" Greybeard asked, his tone rough and unwelcoming as he stepped towards them.

"We're here about the cap in your kitchen," Boubou said confidently.

"What cap? There's no cap in there," Greybeard replied, pretending not to know.

"But there was a cap, a police cap, hanging there when I went to get a drink," Boubou persisted.

"I don't know anything about a cap," Greybeard continued, sticking to his story.

Pierre jumped in, his voice hinting at a warning, "Maybe we should get the police involved and help us figure this out."

At this, Greybeard exchanged a quick, nervous glance with the woman. The other man then stepped forward, trying to take control of the situation.

"That cap he's talking about? It's mine," he claimed boldly. "What's the big deal?"

Boubou didn't back down. "That's not true, and you know it. That cap belongs to the person we're searching for."

The man's face twisted into a snarl, showing yellow teeth. "It's my cap, not a police cap. Don't call me a liar."

At this tense moment, Greybeard stepped forward, hoping to calm things down with a more diplomatic approach. With a hint of resignation in his voice, he addressed the man called Diango. "You're wrong, Diango. I remember the cap they're talking about. I found it on the road a few days back."

"You found it?" Boubou asked, his tone filled with doubt.

"Yeah, found it. A police cap with blood on it," Greybeard admitted.

"That's the cap we're talking about. But why did you hide it when I went to get a drink?" Boubou pressed on.

Greybeard sighed, "Honestly, those bloodstains freaked me out. It's a police cap. I thought it might bring trouble, so I figured it was best to keep it hidden."

"Where exactly did you find it?" Aya interjected, her voice firm.

"About a kilometer from here," Greybeard replied.

"On the shore road?" she pressed further.

"Yes, just lying there in the middle of the road," he confirmed.

"And when was this?" Aya continued her questioning.

"Just a couple of days ago, right after we moved into this place," Greybeard responded, his tone growing tired.

Adama Sambou then stepped in, "Let's see this cap. We need to be sure about your story."

Greybeard, showing a hint of reluctance, started moving towards the kitchen. The woman, meanwhile, sniffed rudely, clearly unimpressed by the turn of events.

The woman's irritation was evident as she voiced her frustration. "Why all this drama over a police cap? You're bothering us at this time of the day, disturbing people who are just trying to live their lives."

Aya responded calmly yet firmly, "We apologize for the disturbance, ma'am. But this issue is important."

At that moment, Greybeard reappeared from the house, holding the cap in his hand. He tossed it toward the group, who immediately gathered around to inspect it.

Boubou carefully turned back the inside flap of the cap, searching for a specific detail. His eyes found what they were looking for—the initials M.G. inked onto the leather band. "This is definitely Chief Gaye's cap," he confirmed.

Aya, peering over Boubou's shoulder, spoke softly, her concern evident. "These bloodstains… they suggest he was seriously injured."

The cap's interior indeed showed signs that its wearer had suffered a severe injury, with extensive bloodstains. The group examined them solemnly, the seriousness of the situation weighing on them.

Boubou, still skeptical, looked up at Greybeard. "Are you absolutely sure you just found this on the road?"

Meeting Boubou's gaze, Greybeard replied defensively, "You think I'd lie about something like this?" His tone implied a challenge as if daring Boubou to dispute his claim further.

"We can't exactly prove you wrong right now. But just so you know, we're handing this cap over to the police. The Chief is missing, and this cap suggests something terrible has happened. If you have any more information, it's best to share it now."

The woman's response was sharp and defensive. "He's told you everything. He found it on the road. Why would he know anything more?"

"We're taking the cap with us," Boubou announced firmly.

"Take it then," Greybeard retorted with a snap, his frustration evident. "I don't want anything to do with it."

Realizing they had gotten all they could from this encounter, the group turned to leave. They had the cap, which was an essential piece of evidence.

In a low voice, Boubou urged, "Let's get out of here."

They returned to the lane, casting a final glance over their shoulders at the house. The woman, Greybeard, and the dark-skinned man remained where the group had left them. The woman stood stiff, hands on her hips, Greybeard with his arms crossed, and the dark-skinned man leaning casually against the car. Their intense, silent stares followed the departing group, a mix of relief and suspicion in their eyes as the kids disappeared from view.

CHAPTER TWELVE

Bypassing The Badge

BACK IN ZINGUICHOU, THE GROUP SAT TOGETHER, EACH DEEP in thought about their visit to Kambossa's house. Everyone was unsatisfied with Greybeard's explanation about the bloodstained police cap they had found.

As usual, Boubou, breaking the silence first, said firmly, "I'm convinced he's hiding something. There's more to his story than he's letting on."

Adama nodded. "Remember how that other guy tried to claim the cap first? Then suddenly, Greybeard comes up with his own story."

"That switch-up was a real red flag," Bacary agreed.

Still puzzled by the discovery, Boubou added, "And why did Greybeard hide the cap when I first went into the kitchen? It doesn't add up."

Aya, ever thoughtful, summed up their concerns. "It's all too weird. Chief Gaye is missing, and then there's this cap with bloodstains…"

Adama, known for his quick decisions, suggested, "We should bring this to Detective Diallo. He's the one who can get to the bottom of this."

The boys exchanged skeptical looks, doubting Detective Diallo's abilities. Known for his tall, slender figure and lack of courage, Diallo wasn't exactly the best Detective. His partner, Officer Boubacar Sarr, wasn't much better, more known for his presence on the streets than any detective abilities. Aya's joke about their combined brainpower only highlighted their doubts. "Put both their brains together, and you'd have enough for a half-wit," she would say.

Boubou, weighing their options, finally spoke up. "I'm not sure Diallo will be much help, but at least it can't hurt. Maybe he can at least scare them with some official questioning."

With that decision, the group made their way to the police station.

They pushed open the front door and marched directly to Chief Gaye's office, not bothering to knock. They found Detective Diallo proudly sitting in the Chief's chair, absorbed in a card game with Constable Sarr.

"It's your move, Sarr," Diallo said, then noticed the group. His face twisted into a mix of surprise and annoyance. "You can't just barge in here, boys!" he exclaimed, trying to maintain an air of authority.

Unfazed, Boubou stepped forward and placed the bloodstained cap on the desk, explaining how they found it. More interested in the game, Sarr scratched his head thoughtfully before triumphantly taking one of Diallo's kings.

Detective Diallo, caught between the card game and the serious matter at hand, grunted. It was unclear if his reaction was due to the loss in the game or the information about the cap.

"So, it's Chief Gaye's cap, is it?" he asked, puffing up his chest and trying to look more authoritative than he felt.

"Yes, it's definitely his," Boubou confirmed.

"And what's your brilliant theory on this?" Diallo smirked.

"We're worried something bad has happened to the Chief, given the state of the cap," Boubou explained. "You did ask us to share our findings with you."

"Just a moment, Sarr — just a moment," Detective Diallo interrupted, focused on his card game. After making his move, he leaned back in the Chief's chair. "Now, try and beat that!" he said, then turned back to the group. "What exactly do you want me to do about this cap?"

"We need help to find Chief Gaye," Boubou said, trying to keep his frustration in check.

Constable Sarr, always dismissive of the kids, interjected with a smirk. "He'll probably turn up in a day or two. He's undercover, right? The note said so. We can't just jump at every kid's hunch."

Diallo, attempting to maintain his composure and appear in control, puffed up his chest, "Imagine, if you will, the Chief on a mission so secret, so utterly important, that the mere flutter of a butterfly's wing could ruin it! To interrupt such a huge task based on the guesses of young detectives-to-be? Ridiculous! It would be like sending a marching band into a library! I will not let the fate of our great city hang in the balance over a hunch. My duty is to protect and uphold the sanctity of our Chief's secret operations. No, no, my dear young friends, I shall not be the one to ruffle the feathers of destiny! I'm not risking my neck over a hunch from you kids."

Aya, undeterred, pressed on. "But he's been missing too long! You need to go to Kambossa's and question those people. They're hiding something about Chief Gaye."

"Kambossa's place, eh?" Diallo said, lips pursing in hesitation. "Well, you see, that's outside our jurisdiction."

"But Chief Gaye is your boss," Aya insisted.

Diallo turned to Sarr. "What do you think, Sarr?"

Focused on the card game, Sarr replied slowly, "Just a moment, it's my move." After playing his card, he looked up. "Honestly, Diallo, I reckon we should avoid Kambossa's. There are some strange tales about that place."

"Exactly," Diallo hastily agreed, clearly eager to avoid any potential danger.

Boubou, visibly frustrated, asked, "So, you're not even going to try to help us find him?"

Trying to sound confident, Diallo replied, "We'll keep an eye out, but don't worry. He'll turn up soon. You'll see."

Aya, unconvinced and a bit heated, retorted, "He'll never show up if we're waiting for the Zinguichou Police to take the lead."

"Is that so?" Diallo replied, clearly ruffled by her remark.

Boubou, seizing the moment with a hint of sarcasm, said smoothly, "Of course, Detective. If the thought of visiting Kambossa's, what with its spooky reputation, is too much for you, we understand. We'll just let the newspapers know that we suspect foul play in Chief Gaye's disappearance, but the local police are too... preoccupied to investigate. Don't let us interrupt your card game, though."

"What's this about the newspapers?" Detective Diallo blurted, jumping up so quickly that the cards scattered across Sarr's lap. The fear of any unflattering publicity, a constant concern for the police, was evident in his panicked tone.

Aya's suggestion hit a nerve. "If the taxpayers knew you were too scared to investigate Kambossa's place, they might not be too happy. They do pay for law enforcement, after all."

Detective Diallo, visibly flustered, tried to regain control of the situation. "Whoa, whoa, let's not get ahead of ourselves. Afraid of Kambossa's? Me? Nonsense! I was just joking around. Of course, I'll go up and check this out. Well—at least I'll send Sarr up—"

Sarr, who had been trying to gather the scattered cards, looked up in shock. "Wait, what? Me?"

"Yes, Sarr. We're a team," Diallo stated, trying to sound convincing.

"I'm definitely not heading up there alone," Sarr asserted firmly.

Boubou decided to ease off, sensing they had pushed the right buttons. "As long as you're committed to investigating, we'll keep quiet about this to the press."

Detective Diallo, relieved, quickly agreed. "Absolutely, absolutely. Sarr and I, too, will head up there first thing tomorrow morning. If we find anything, you'll be the first to know." His tone was a mix of eagerness to please and a hint of desperation to keep the matter out of the public eye.

The next morning, Boubou and Aya, determined to follow up on the investigation, arrived at the station, hoping for some solid information from Detectives Diallo and Sarr. However, their hopes were quickly crushed.

Despite their apparent lack of enthusiasm, Diallo and Sarr had duly left Zinguichou in an exceptionally noisy and beat-up old car, with Sarr nervously sitting at the wheel. By midday, they were back, reporting that their investigation had hit a dead end.

"We visited the house, but the people living there gave a believable story of how they found the cap," Diallo said. "They insisted they found it on the road. Why would they lie? So, we saw no reason to stay."

Sarr, echoing his partner's words, added thoughtfully, "Yes, we left."

"In a hurry, I bet," Aya said, her voice dripping with sarcasm.

Diallo and Sarr shifted uncomfortably in their seats. The truth was, they had been so spooked by the creepy stories about Kambossa's house that they barely stayed long. They asked only a few basic questions, accepted Greybeard's explanation without much digging, and left as soon as it seemed polite to do so.

"We've done what we could," Detective Diallo declared, trying to sound confident. "A man can do no more than that."

Boubou and Aya exchanged a glance, their disappointment clear. They realized this was as much as they could expect from the local police. Resigned, they left the station, their minds racing about what to do next.

Unsatisfied with the police's half-hearted investigation, Boubou and Aya stood by their bikes on the sidewalk outside the station, their minds deep in thought over the unfolding mystery.

Aya, putting together the clues, confidently said, "There's definitely a connection between the smuggling ring and Kambossa's house. I bet Scorpion is right in the middle of it all."

"Isn't Scorpion related to Kambossa?" Boubou remembered, trying to connect the dots.

"Yes, and it makes sense that he'd inherit Kambossa's house after the old man died," Aya guessed. "That could be why he's moved his smuggling activities to this area."

"That's a strong possibility," Boubou agreed. "And remember the two men at the house? Scorpion could have been one of them."

Aya nodded. "Wouldn't surprise me at all. But there's another thing that's bothering me. Where did those two motorboats come from the day Hounsou was shot? We didn't see them in the bay. They seemed to appear from beneath the cliffs."

"You think there's a hidden harbor there?" Boubou thought about the idea.

"It's a possible theory," Aya replied.

"Scorpion was involved in Hounsou's attack," Boubou continued. "He's connected to Kambossa, and he's been running a smuggling operation that no one's been able to trace. Maybe the base of his operations is actually Kambossa's house, hidden in plain sight."

"Except the house is at the top of a cliff. Not too practical for unloading goods," Aya remarked.

"But what if there's a secret passageway leading from the house down to a hidden harbor at the base of the cliff?"

Aya's eyes widened. "Wow, Boubou, that actually sounds possible!"

"And think about it," Boubou continued, "this could explain how the kidnappers vanished with Hounsou so fast. If they had headed towards Kambossa's after leaving the Touma salt farm, it makes sense why we lost track of them. We should have caught a glimpse, but we didn't."

"You think they might have taken shelter at Kambossa's?" Aya asked, piecing the puzzle together.

"It's a strong possibility. Hounsou might still be there, hidden… unless they've hurt him," Boubou said, a hint of worry in his voice.

"But where does that leave Chief Gaye?" Aya wondered aloud.

Boubou had a plan. "Let's see if Pierre's dad will let us use his motorboat to check out the base of the cliff."

"What are you hoping to find?" Aya asked, curious about the next step.

Boubou's determination was evident. "If there's a spot where boats can be hidden, we'll find it. Any solid evidence we gather, we can hand it over to the government authorities. A raid on Kambossa's place could provide some answers, maybe even lead us to Chief Gaye."

* * *

CHAPTER THIRTEEN

Unwelcome Waters

THE DIOUF SIBLINGS, FILLED WITH EXCITEMENT AND determination, shared their daring plan with Pierre. His response was enthusiastic and immediate, his adventurous spirit shining through.

"I wouldn't miss this for the world," he declared with a grin. "Just make sure I'm part of this adventure, and I'll make sure we have the boat. It's a deal."

Boubou, recognizing the value of having Pierre on board, quickly agreed. "We wouldn't even think of going without you, Pierre," he assured.

Pierre, thrilled to be included, laid out the plan. "I'll get the boat ready by tomorrow afternoon. Meet me at the harbor—that's where our expedition begins." The team, now a trio, was set, and the anticipation for the next day was palpable.

❖

Per his promise, Pierre was ready and waiting for Boubou and Aya at the harbor. The siblings found him at one of the run-down docks that lined the shore, absorbed in his work. Dressed in greasy overalls, Pierre was bent over the boat's engine, his hands skillfully making adjustments. His fascination with mechanics was unmistakable; he had a natural talent for understanding and fixing machinery.

"She's going to run smoother than a sewing machine," Pierre announced confidently, a hint of pride in his voice as he looked up from the engine. "We're all set to go whenever you're ready."

"Your dad didn't mind lending us the boat?" Boubou asked, impressed by Pierre's handiwork.

"Not at all," Pierre replied. "I mentioned it was to find Chief Gaye. He was so into the idea that he almost dropped everything to join us!"

The three friends boarded the motorboat, a sleek and powerful vessel that belied its name, 'Riviera,' a nod to Mr. Laporte's French origins. Once everyone was settled, Pierre revved the engine, and the boat began to hum to life. They eased out of the harbor, the Riviera cutting through the water gracefully. As they moved further into the bay, the engine roared louder, and the boat picked up speed, heading towards the ominous cliffs at the northern edge of Zinguichou Bay. The adventure was truly underway.

The sky grew increasingly cloudy as the afternoon went on, casting a somber mood over Zinguichou Bay. With its trio of young adventurers, the Riviera braved the choppy waters, the salt spray crashing over its bows as it forged ahead through the waves. The familiar outline of Zinguichou faded into a hazy blur behind them while the white streak of the shore road weaved along the coast to the north. Soon, the Touma salt farm came into view, its ponds glinting amidst the rocky landscape.

The cliff, where Kambossa's house perched ominously, loomed ahead, a stark, imposing presence outlined against the vast ocean and cloudy sky. They could make out the grove of baobabs atop the cliff surrounding the house, its roof and chimneys just visible.

Aya peered at the scene. "Such a lonely-looking place," she remarked, her voice tinged with awe and unease.

Pierre, focusing on the steepness of the cliff, noted, "It's hard to imagine anyone climbing up or down that slope to reach the house."

"That's exactly why it's perfect for smuggling," Boubou thought. "It seems impossible, which might be why nobody has suspected it. But we might find things are different once we look closer."

Carefully, Pierre maneuvered the boat closer to shore, keeping it out of sight from anyone who might be at Kambossa's. He then reduced the engine's roar to a gentle hum, allowing the Riviera to glide more quietly along the cliff base.

Navigating the currents near the cliff demanded Pierre's full attention and skill, but he efficiently handled the Riviera. The boat edged closer to the cliff face, allowing them a clear view of the rugged rock wall. It was deeply scarred and worn, the base showing signs of years of relentless wave assault.

Time ticked by as they scanned the cliff for any signs of a hidden path or entrance. Despite their keen observation, there was no obvious indication of a secret harbor or access point. Disappointment began to set in among the young sleuths as the reality of their challenging quest became clear.

The Riviera was navigating dangerous waters, with the cliff towering like a guard above them. From their position, Kambossa's place remained hidden, its location set just back from the cliff's edge, making it invisible from the water. The cliff presented a scary sight—a sheer, rocky face offering no obvious paths or entrances, seemingly impossible to climb.

Suddenly, Pierre's hands spun the wheel. The boat lurched to the side, its engine roaring to life as it surged forward. Boubou and Aya, startled by the sudden move, looked around in confusion and alarm.

"What's happening?" they asked simultaneously, their voices tinged with concern.

Pierre's eyes locked on the path ahead was the picture of concentration and urgency. With another quick twist of the wheel, the Riviera veered sharply once again.

It was then that the siblings spotted the immediate danger. Sharp, jagged rocks lurked menacingly through the water's surface, resembling the scary teeth of some sea monster. One particularly evil-looking rock stuck out dangerously close to their boat. Pierre's keen observation and quick reflexes had narrowly avoided a collision.

They found themselves in the middle of a dangerous field of reefs, extending several meters ahead, hidden threats lurking just below the waterline. Every heartbeat felt loud as they held their breath, the Riviera carefully navigating through the hazardous maze, guided by Pierre's steady hand and sharp eyes.

The tension aboard the Riviera was evident as they continued to navigate through the dangerous rock-filled waters. The possibility of hitting a hidden reef and damaging the boat was on their minds, but Pierre's skillful steering kept them safe. His quick handling of the boat, weaving through the treacherous rocks, was nothing short of amazing.

Miraculously, they managed to avoid every visible danger. With one final, nimble move, Pierre steered the Riviera past the last threatening rock, propelling them into the safety of open water. He relaxed visibly, letting out a sigh full of relief.

"Whew, that was close!" Pierre exclaimed, the strain in his voice unmistakable. "I didn't even see those rocks until we were almost on them. Hitting one would have been disastrous."

Boubou and Aya nodded in agreement, fully aware of the risk they had just escaped. The furious waves crashing against the cliff's base were a stark reminder of what could have been their fate—a merciless battering against the unforgiving rocks.

Just as they processed their narrow escape, something unexpected caught their attention. Ahead of them, an opening appeared on the side of the cliff—a long, narrow cove hidden from view until one was almost upon it. The discovery was startling, and it instantly reignited their sense of purpose. Could this be the secret access they were searching for?

The possibility sent a ripple of excitement through the trio as they approached the mysterious cove. As they neared the cove, its entrance appeared daunting, resembling the narrow neck of a bottle flanked by overhanging rocks. The cove's clever concealment was apparent—it was practically invisible until one was right upon it and just as quickly hidden again from a slight distance.

Boubou couldn't contain his excitement. "This could be huge! Let's check it out," he urged, his eyes sparkling with the thrill of discovery.

With a nod of determination, Pierre carefully maneuvered the Riviera back towards the cove. As they approached again, the opening revealed itself, a secret passage waiting to be explored.

"It looks just big enough for the boat," Pierre observed, his tone cautious yet curious. "Shall we go in?"

Boubou's response was immediate. "Yes, let's do it."

Sitting beside Boubou, Aya added, "We have to see where it leads. This could be the clue we've been looking for."

As the boat inched closer to the mysterious bay, Pierre suddenly expressed concern: "What if we can't turn back once we're in there?"

Aya tried to reassure him, "We'll be fine. If it gets too tight, we can always back out slowly."

His worry was short-lived, though. As they entered, the cove opened into a wider bay, offering ample space for maneuvering.

"Wow, this place is amazing," Aya exclaimed, looking around at the hidden bay.

Reassured, Pierre continued onwards, guiding the Riviera deeper into the cove. "Looks like we have plenty of space to turn around if we need to," he said, more relaxed now.

Boubou leaned over the edge of the boat, peering into the water. "Keep your eyes peeled for anything unusual," he said. "We might find more than just a hidden cove."

Aya nodded, her eyes scanning the shoreline. "I wonder if there's an entrance to a cave or something."

Unexpectedly, the Riviera eased into a hidden bay that was far more expansive than they had anticipated. The bay, a secret sanctuary carved into the cliff, was calm and sheltered, starkly contrasting with the choppy waters they had just navigated. Its walls rose steeply, creating an isolated and secluded area.

As they ventured deeper, the trio was struck by the surreal quietness of the place, a hidden world away from the open sea. The water was clear, and the light that filtered in from the entrance cast eerie shadows on the rocky walls. The bay was deep enough to accommodate the boat easily, and Pierre skillfully steered the Riviera to a gentle float in the middle of this secret cove.

Boubou, Aya, and Pierre exchanged glances of awe and excitement. This discovery could be the key to unraveling the mysteries they were pursuing. The possibility that they had stumbled upon the secret base of the smuggling operation seemed increasingly likely.

"Could this be where they've been hiding the boats?" Aya whispered, her voice echoing softly against the rocky walls.

"It's perfect for smuggling," Boubou thought. "Hidden, accessible by sea, and impossible to spot from the land or even the air."

Pierre kept a steady hand on the wheel, eyes scanning the cove for any sign of activity or further clues. "Let's take a closer look around," he suggested.

The Riviera drifted slowly, the trio's eyes searching the bay's edges. If there were any signs of recent activity or hidden passageways leading further into the cliff, they were determined to find them.

At first glance, the cove seemed like nothing special. Its sides were very steep, with dense bushes huddling at the foot of the slopes. Still, it lacked signs of human presence—no paths, no trails, nothing to suggest anyone had ever set foot there. Sheltered from the wind, the water lay still and serene, the motorboat's engine sounds echoing loudly, bouncing off the slopes in a thunderous chorus.

Then, out of the blue, Boubou let out a startled gasp. "Whoa, check that out!"

Among the bushes at the base of the steepest slope stood a man. He was a towering figure, wearing a black felt hat with a wide brim that cast a shadow over his eyes. His face, dark and weather-worn, was marked by thin, harsh lips. Dressed in a short black jacket, his hands were buried in his pockets, and his stance was wide, like a sailor bracing against a stormy sea.

He just stood there, eerily still, his gaze fixed on them without a flicker of emotion, resembling a sinister statue.

Noticing he had caught their attention, he bellowed, "Get out of here!"

Pierre, a bit shaken, eased off the boat's engine. The three of them—Pierre, Boubou, and Aya—couldn't help but stare at the man in the black hat as if he were some sort of ghostly vision.

"I said, leave!" His voice was oddly metallic, like the clang of a bell.

"But we're not causing any trouble," Boubou protested defiantly.

"Not yet," the stranger retorted sharply. "But don't you dare land here."

"Why can't we?" Boubou asked.

"You don't need a reason. This is private property. You're not allowed to land. You better skedaddle, and fast," the man in the black hat replied tersely.

The kids exchanged uncertain glances. To underline his point, the man suddenly reached into his pocket and flashed a menacing revolver. He then crossed his arms, tapping the gun barrel against his shoulder with a deliberate rhythm.

"Turn this boat around and scram!" he barked. "And don't think of coming back. Ever. Try to land here again, and you'll be met with bullets."

The kids were clearly outmatched. They knew arguing would get them nowhere. Pierre obediently steered the boat to leave.

"See ya!" Aya called out, her voice surprisingly cheerful under the circumstances.

The stranger didn't respond. He just stood there, his eyes following them, still tapping the revolver against his shoulder as the motorboat retreated from the mysterious cove into the open waters.

"Seems like he really didn't want us there," Pierre observed once they were safely away.

"You're telling me!" Boubou exclaimed. "That guy looked dangerous. I half expected him to start shooting at us before we were clear."

"I definitely don't want to bump into him again," Pierre said firmly.

"He was pretty clear with his warning, and he meant every word," Boubou added.

"Who could he be?" Pierre wondered aloud.

"Do you think—hey, guys! Could that have been Scorpion?" Aya suddenly blurted out, her voice rising with excitement and a hint of fear.

Boubou Diouf's mind raced as the realization hit him, sharp and unexpected like lightning in a clear sky. The stranger's entrance had been nothing short of scary—a shadowy figure giving off a sense of danger and command, his ties to Kambossa's house all too obvious and ominous.

"Scorpion!" Aya blurted out, her voice tinged with certainty. "It has to be him."

"The boss of the smugglers," Boubou nodded in agreement.

Aya's brows furrowed in thought. "I've never seen a photo of Scorpion, nor have I heard anyone describe him," she said. "But this guy, he's exactly like the Scorpion I've imagined in my wildest dreams."

Pierre, always the observant one, added his thoughts. "He's definitely a leader, no doubt about it. His aura, his attitude, it screams authority."

"He's the same one who gave Hounsou a run for his money that day with the speedboat," Boubou recalled, a hint of worry in his voice.

Pierre's eyes widened. "And if we hang around here much longer, we'll be the next ones he's chasing," he warned.

Their eyes met, a silent agreement passing between them. It was time to act, and quickly.

"Why bail out now?" Boubou challenged. "This could be a major find. Maybe it's the smugglers' hideout."

Pierre scratched his head, skeptical. "But how would they move between here and Kambossa's? Those cliffs aren't exactly a walk in the park."

Boubou's eyes gleamed with intent. "There's got to be a route we're missing. How about we stick around and do a little Detective work?"

Soon enough, Pierre was caught in the Dioufs' adventurous spirit. They decided to keep their motorboat nearby, but not too close—just in case the man with the piercing gaze was on the lookout. They'd cruise along the shore, casual but alert.

"Good thing we didn't stir things up with that guy," Boubou finally said, a hint of relief in his voice.

Pierre nodded vigorously. "Absolutely! With that revolver of his, arguing wasn't exactly an option."

Boubou smirked. "Not just that. He might think we were just cruising around and accidentally stumbled into that cove. If he guessed we're onto the Chief, things might have gotten real ugly real fast."

Aya chimed in, her voice determined. "Exactly. We're not heading home just yet. We've got more ground to cover."

❖

As the day approached evening, the sky, covered in gray clouds, showed that night was coming soon. A cold wind blew across them, smelling of salt from the sea. Their motorboat, looking tiny against the vast shoreline, moved skillfully under Pierre's guidance. They turned away from the shore, then came back, staying a safe distance from the bay. Their eyes kept watching the cove's location, which, even though they knew exactly where it was, was hard to see—just a tiny crack in the big rock wall.

Looking out into the distance, Boubou was amazed at how well it was hidden. "No wonder this place is so mysterious," he thought out loud. "From here, it looks like just one solid wall of rock."

Holding onto the boat's side, Aya called out warningly. "Careful, Pierre! We're getting too close to danger here. One wrong move, and we could crash into those rocks."

Boubou nodded in agreement, his eyes scanning the dangerous cliffs nearby. "Yeah, we've got to stay alert. It's tricky water here."

Pierre, confident in his skills, reassured them. "Just trust me. I've got this boat under control."

Indeed, Pierre was good with the motorboat, but the sea was unpredictable. They came close to trouble several times, with waves crashing hard against the rocks. At one point, a sudden bump followed by a scraping sound made them all gasp, their hearts racing for a moment.

"That was a close one, for sure," Pierre admitted, sounding a bit more humble. "Maybe staying a bit further from the edge is smarter."

"I'd say so," Boubou agreed, his voice showing relief and caution.

They kept watching from the water, the motorboat carefully moving along the shoreline. Even after spending over an hour keeping watch, everything stayed weirdly quiet. There wasn't even the slightest sign of movement, not at the bottom of the cliff or around Kambossa's property, which they could clearly see from their safer, more distant spot out at sea.

As the evening shadows grew longer, Boubou, Aya, and Pierre started to feel like their efforts might be useless. But Boubou, always optimistic, wasn't ready to give up yet.

"Remember, these guys don't usually work in daylight. Night is their time," Boubou reminded them, his voice steady and convincing. "Let's stick around a bit longer."

As night fell, the distant lights of Zinguichou made a faint, yellow glow through the mist at the far end of the bay. The cliff became just a shadow, its outline blurry in the darkness, while the waves crashed against the rocks, making the only steady sound in the quiet night.

Then, breaking through the silence, came a muffled noise. The kids turned off their engine, letting their boat glide quietly, straining to hear in the darkness.

"Another boat," Pierre whispered, his voice very quiet.

Indeed, another motorboat was hovering near the bottom of the cliff. A faint light flickered in the distance, and they carefully steered their boat towards it, hearts pounding with excitement.

The tension was high as they moved forward slowly, knowing that the next few moments could be crucial. Coming from the west, they didn't dare get too close, but close enough to see the dark shape of the other boat as it slowly came out from the cliff itself, like a ghost in the night.

They were puzzled by why the other boat was so close to the shore. They moved closer, fully aware of the risks—they could be spotted or crash into the sharp rocks. As they got nearer, they heard the other boat's engine slowing down, followed by the unmistakable sound of oars and muffled voices.

Then, without warning, the other motorboat roared to life, startling them. It sped away into the bay, its engine getting fainter as it headed out to sea.

"Where's it going?" Pierre wondered.

Boubou quickly shushed him, his eyes scanning the darkness.

"There's a rowboat out here," he whispered urgently. "Stay quiet."

They held their breath, feeling tense in the still night air. Soon, they could clearly hear the sound of oars moving through the water, getting louder with each stroke.

The rowboat was coming closer.

Luckily, the wind was blowing from the sea towards them. It carried the sounds to them while hiding the gentle hum of their own boat, protecting them from being heard by the unseen rowers in the darkness.

The rhythmic splash of oars cutting through the water grew more precise, and soon, they could see the shadowy outline of the rowboat in the dim light. Straining their ears, Boubou, Aya, and Pierre tried to catch the conversation of the figures hidden in the boat's darkness. At Boubou's signal, Pierre turned off the engine, plunging them into a tense silence.

They could only hear bits and pieces of the conversation, with the wind carrying some words to them and the rest being lost in the night.

"—three hundred rocks—" a harsh voice said, but the rest was lost in the wind.

The voices continued, a dull, unclear murmur until another fragment reached them.

"I don't know. It's risky—"

The wind paused momentarily, and in that brief quiet, the trio saw the rowboat steering straight for the cliff face, only a few yards away now. As it glided past, they heard the harsh voice again.

"Colonel Parker's share—" he stated.

"No, we mustn't forget that," another gruff voice responded.

"I hope they get away all right."

"Why worry? Of course they'll get away."

"But we've been watched, you know."

"That's all in your head. No one suspects a thing."

"Those young ones at the house—"

"They're just kids. If they get in the way again, we'll handle them," said the cold, threatening voice.

The second man voiced his concern, "I don't like where this is going. It's getting risky."

"In our line of work, you can't afford to be soft. What's gotten into you tonight? You seem on edge," the first man retorted sharply.

"I've got this bad feeling… Maybe we should pack up and leave."

"Leave? You've got to be kidding," the first man scoffed. "This place is as secure as it gets. We're invisible here. We'll make our fortune before anyone even realizes we're here."

"Well, perhaps you're right," the second man agreed hesitantly, though uncertainty lingered in his voice.

Their conversation faded into the night as their boat disappeared into the cove. The sound of their oars was followed by a rustling of bushes, a final muffled remark, and then nothing but silence.

Boubou, Aya, and Pierre exchanged worried glances in the dim light.

"Smugglers," Boubou whispered, his voice revealing fear but excitement.

"It sure seems like it," Pierre whispered back. "What's our next move?"

Boubou's eyes were determined. "We follow them."

Aya's agreement was instant, her voice filled with the thrill of the chase. "Right, we follow them to their hideout."

Pierre, however, was more cautious. He started the engine again, but his words showed hesitation. "I'm not so sure," he said. "That bit about 'handling' the kids doesn't sound good. I'm adventurous, not reckless."

Boubou argued, "But there's three of us."

"And who knows how many of them," Pierre shot back. "They're adults, and we're just kids. "Getting cornered in that cove? Not a great idea. Plus, this motorboat isn't quiet—they'll hear us coming."

The Diouf siblings had to admit Pierre's point was valid. The idea of sneaking into the cove, especially in darkness and with the noisy motorboat, was hazardous.

Boubou sighed, the frustration evident in his voice. "It's tough to let them slip away, especially now that we're onto something big. They're definitely smugglers. The guys on that motorboat might be heading out to a ship to pick up or drop off smuggled goods."

Aya's curiosity then took over. "But where did that motorboat come from in the first place? We didn't see any boat in the cove when we were there earlier."

"They've likely got it well hidden," Boubou said. "Remember the thick bushes near the water's edge? Perfect for hiding a boat."

"But where did those men come from?" Aya pressed on, still puzzled.

"That," Boubou stated firmly, "is exactly what we need to find out. There's got to be a connection between this cove and Kambossa's place. I'm going ashore to check it out."

Pierre, though reluctant, acknowledged the necessity of their plan. "Someone needs to stay with the motorboat," he said. "I'm not scared to go in, and I would if it were a challenge, but we can't just leave the boat here."

Boubou quickly made a plan. "Here's what we'll do. Aya and I will go ashore and track those men. If we lose them now, we might never find them again."

"And what about me?" Pierre asked.

"You head back to Zinguichou and bring back help," Boubou instructed. "And I mean a lot of help."

"The police?" asked Pierre.

Boubou nodded, his decision firm. "We need to contact the government agents in Zakar. We're in over our heads. It's time to bring in the authorities. This is bigger than us." Boubou's voice carried a sense of urgency and determination. "If they're tracking this 'Scorpion' character, they must have operatives nearby. Tell them we're hot on the smugglers' trail. If Aya and I find something, we'll wait at the cove's entrance and guide the police when they arrive."

Pierre nodded, anxiety and resolve visible in his eyes. "Okay, let's do this. I'll get you two ashore right now."

"But not too close—we can't risk damaging the boat. Looks like it's a swim for us, Aya."

With careful precision, Pierre maneuvered the boat as close to the scary shoreline as possible. Then, in a hushed goodbye, Boubou and Aya plunged into the cool, dark waters. Only a few yards from the rocks, their swim was short but intense. Soaked but determined, they climbed onto the shore, turning back just in time to see the vague outline of the motorboat as it turned away, the muffled sound of its engine fading into the distance towards Zinguichou.

The plan was set. Boubou turned to Aya, his voice barely above a whisper in the quiet of the night. "Now! Let's find those smugglers!"

CHAPTER FOURTEEN

Into The Smuggler's Lair

Under the cover of darkness, Aya whispered, breaking the silence. "I wish we had some light."

Boubou, always prepared, replied quietly, "I've got Dad's old flashlight, but we can't risk using it. Those guys might still be around."

Aya asked, "Did the water damage it?"

"No, it's safe in a waterproof case. Let's just feel our way around these rocks until we reach the cove."

They carefully made their way over the rocky ground. Aya stumbled once, splashing into the water. They froze, hearts racing, worried they had alerted the men in the cove. But the night stayed quiet.

Wet but determined, Aya climbed back onto the rocky path. The cove entrance was only about 80 feet away, but the dangerous rocks and the tension of their mission made it feel much farther.

As they inched forward, Boubou whispered, "This has to be Scorpion and his gang. Did you catch that American name one of them mentioned?"

Aya nodded, remembering the snippet of conversation. "Yeah, something about Colonel Parker's share."

"That's it," Boubou said thoughtfully. "Colonel Parker might be the guy bringing in blood diamonds. They smuggle them here by boat, then distribute them from this cove. Dad said Scorpion was into drug smuggling too."

"The guy who chased us off earlier," Aya added, "he seemed like the boss. Probably Scorpion himself."

Boubou's voice held a mix of excitement and seriousness. "Can you imagine? A $50,000 reward for catching him!"

As they neared the cove's entrance, relief washed over them. The cliffs, which they had worried might be too steep, gradually sloped down to the water, offering a narrow but walkable ledge.

Stepping onto this ledge, they knew they were starting the most dangerous part of their journey. The cliffs cast long shadows, making the loneliness more intense. The distant sound of the ocean and the steady crashing of waves against the reefs added to the spooky atmosphere. Far away, the lights of Zinguichou twinkled through the mist, reminding them of the world beyond their current danger. Every so often, they heard the faint hum of Pierre's motorboat as he traveled down the bay, a distant but comforting link to safety.

Boubou, full of anticipation, said, "I hope the agents come prepared—with lights, guns, everything."

Aya asked curiously, "Who are you talking about?"

"The government agents," he explained. "Trust me, if they hear Scorpion's been found, they'll send an army, not just a few guys."

The thick bushes loomed large as they rounded the bend into the cove. Dense plants stretched to the water's edge, creating a natural hiding place that could easily conceal danger. The thought that the men from the boat might be hiding nearby, ready to ambush them, sent chills down their spines. Despite the obvious risk, they never considered turning back. Their mission was bigger than just smugglers; they were also there for Chief Gaye.

Reaching the first cluster of bushes, they paused, knowing any sound could give them away. The snapping of twigs under their feet seemed as loud as thunder in the quiet night. They hesitated briefly, wondering what to do next. Then, with a determined whisper, Boubou suggested a bold plan.

"Let's try wading around," he whispered, slowly lowering himself off the rock into the water. "If it's not too deep, we can sneak around without being noticed."

Luckily, the water was shallow, barely reaching Boubou's knees. He motioned for Aya to join him, and she slid into the water silently, barely making a ripple.

Together, they moved extremely slowly, wading through the cool water and ducking under the overhanging branches that lined the cove's edge. It felt like they were exploring the bottom of a hidden pit, with towering rock walls surrounding them, creating a world cut off from everything else. As they went deeper, they could no longer see the cove's entrance, hidden by the curves of the cliff. Above them, only a thin strip of the night sky was visible, a grey expanse that seemed both far away and close at hand.

The cove was eerily quiet, making Boubou and Aya think the men from the boat had hidden somewhere. Realizing they couldn't go further without light, Boubou carefully removed the flashlight from its waterproof case and turned it on.

The beam cut through the darkness, lighting up the pale leaves along the shore and creating sharp shadows on the rocky walls. Boubou swept the light around, checking every corner of the cove. But no matter how hard they looked, there was no sign of the rowboat the men had used. It had vanished like magic.

The siblings were ready for surprises but hadn't expected the boat to disappear completely. They searched the area thoroughly, but the flashlight showed nothing but rocks and plants.

"Where could they have hidden it?" Boubou whispered, mostly to himself.

They kept searching, carefully combing through the thick bushes around the cove. They moved as quietly as they could, but all they found were more bushes and mossy rocks.

"It must be a cave or something," Boubou decided. "That's where they must be hiding."

Determined to find answers, they kept looking, still wading through the cold water that made their legs numb. They pushed branches aside and checked every possible hiding spot, but the cove seemed determined to keep its secrets.

Then, as they reached a new part of the cove, Boubou suddenly lost his footing. Instead of solid ground, his foot found empty space, and he fell forward. But even as he fell, he quickly held the flashlight up high to keep it dry as he plunged into deeper water up to his neck.

He had stumbled into a hidden deep spot. Even though he was underwater and struggling to stand up, his main worry was keeping the flashlight, their only light source, from getting wet.

"Here! Grab the light," he managed to whisper hoarsely.

Aya quickly leaned over and grabbed the flashlight.

"Deepwater here," Boubou muttered, trying hard to return to the shallow area.

The sudden drop made it tough for him to get back. Aya had to reach out and grab her brother's hand to help him find his footing. Finally, both soaking wet and shivering, Boubou stood beside Aya again.

"That was close," he said, catching his breath. "The water's been pretty shallow until now. It's weird to have such a deep spot suddenly."

Then, Boubou had a lightbulb moment. "I get it now," he whispered excitedly. "That's not just a hole. It's a channel. Can you see how it runs close to the shore? The water's deeper here than it should be."

Aya looked confused. "But why a channel?"

"It's for the boats—the motorboat and the rowboat," Boubou figured out. "They'd need deeper water to reach the shore without getting stuck. Give me the light. I think we're close to finding where they've been hiding that boat."

As Aya returned the flashlight to Boubou, everything started to make sense. The mysterious deep spot and the hidden channel were all part of a clever secret path that the smugglers had made for their sneaky operations.

The flashlight beam, now steady in Boubou's hand, showed the actual shape of the cove's bottom. A deep, narrow channel cut through the floor, winding toward some bushes at the water's edge. This hidden waterway led straight to something they couldn't see yet.

Carefully avoiding the deeper channel, Boubou and Aya approached the thick bushes. The flashlight beam pierced through the leaves, revealing the secret they'd been looking for—a dark opening in the rock.

"A cave!" Boubou whispered, his voice full of wonder and triumph.

The cave entrance was so well hidden that it would have been nearly impossible to spot in daylight. But now, lit up by their flashlight, it stood out clearly against the dense plants.

This was the missing piece of the puzzle. The channel in the cove let the smugglers steer their boats right into this hidden cave. It explained how the motorboat and rowboat seemed to appear and disappear like magic.

"They went in here," Aya said quietly but firmly.

Boubou nodded, his mind made up. "We're going in to explore."

The decision was made; there was no turning back now. Boubou and Aya, driven by bravery and curiosity, were determined to solve the mystery inside the cave. The dark, unknown calling from the cave's mouth held secrets they were set on uncovering, even if it might be dangerous.

They pushed forward, fighting through the thick bushes that seemed to try to keep them out.

"Watch your step, Aya," Boubou said, holding a branch out of her way.

"I'm trying," Aya replied, her voice strained as she ducked under another branch. "These bushes are relentless!"

Branches cracked, and leaves rustled as they pushed through, the plants brushing against their faces and leaving little signs that someone had passed by.

"Almost there," Boubou encouraged, his tone determined. "Just a little further."

Luckily, the water stayed shallow along the narrow edge next to the channel, thanks to the low tide. This natural path gave them just enough room to move forward without having to wade into deeper water.

"Good thing the tide's low," Boubou remarked, glancing at the water. "We'd be in deeper water otherwise."

Finally, they broke free from the grabbing branches and leaves. The bushes closed up behind them, shutting off the outside world. Now, they stood at the entrance of a hidden passage, the mouth of the cave, pressing against its cold, wet walls.

"Whoa," Aya breathed, her eyes wide as she took in the sight. "This is incredible."

The air smelled strongly of sea and dirt. Their flashlight beam, their only light, cut through the darkness, showing a path that led deep into the cave.

✳ ✳ ✳

CHAPTER FIFTEEN

In The Heart Of The Cliff

B OUBOU TURNED ON THE FLASHLIGHT, CUTTING THROUGH the thick darkness around them. The light beam stretched far into the shadowy tunnel, showing a dull, grey shape floating just above the water's surface in the distance.

"What's that?" Aya whispered, squinting into the gloom.

For a moment, they were surprised. Then they realized what it was—the same rowboat they had seen earlier, disappearing into the night outside the hidden bay. Now, it rested near a natural dock carved right out of the cliff, gently bouncing on the water.

"It's the rowboat from before!" Boubou exclaimed softly. "Looks like we were right about this place."

Carefully, Boubou and Aya made their way along the narrow ledge. It was just wide enough for one person, so they had to watch their step until the path slowly got wider, leading straight to the makeshift dock. Everything was quiet except for the occasional drip of water echoing off the gloomy walls.

"Watch your step," Boubou cautioned, keeping his voice low. "This ledge is pretty dodgy."

"I got it," Aya replied, carefully placing each foot on the rocky path.

They crept across the dock, passing by the boat, their eyes carefully scanning everything around them. Boubou swept the flashlight beam across the cave, the light bouncing off rocks and cracks. Suddenly, the bright light revealed a spooky opening right before them. Framed by a rough stone arch, a steep wooden staircase entered the unknown, inviting them into the heart of the cliff's mystery.

Aya's heart was pounding, a mix of nerves and excitement rushing through her. They had stumbled onto something big, something secret.

"We did it," she whispered, nudging Boubou. "This is it, the hidden passage. It's got to be right under Kambossa's place."

"Easy there, keep it down," Boubou whispered back. "We need to be careful and move quietly."

The flashlight beam made weird, dancing shadows in the dark corridor. Drops of water fell from the walls, landing on their already damp clothes.

They tiptoed forward, ducking under the arch to reach the staircase. Then, moving as quietly as cats, they started climbing up, each step showing how good they were at being sneaky.

"Do you think anyone's up there?" Aya whispered, glancing up the steep staircase.

"Could be," Boubou answered. "Just stay close and be ready for anything."

Their footsteps were soft, almost soundless, as they ascended, the mystery of the hidden passage pulling them deeper into the heart of the cliff.

❖

It was so quiet that they felt like they had stepped into a forgotten world, like an ancient tomb. The stairs were so silent and untouched that it barely looked like anyone had used them, even though Boubou and Aya knew smugglers must have been here not long ago.

They carefully climbed up, the flashlight showing the way until it finally lit up a door. The door was set into the rock wall at the top of the stairs, looking like a big question mark at the end of their journey. The passage above curved in the natural shape of the cliff.

Stopping at the top step, just outside the door, Aya whispered, "Should we go in?"

They didn't know what was waiting for them on the other side. Could it be where the smugglers hid out? It seemed likely. And if so, they might be walking into a trap with no way out.

They hesitated for a moment, thinking about what to do. Should they go back or keep going?

Boubou then took a bold step forward. "Hold on," he whispered. He put his ear against the door and listened really hard. Nothing. He looked around the edges of the door, searching for any bit of light. It was all dark.

Deciding it was safe, at least for now, he turned to Aya. "We're going in," he whispered, sounding determined.

Aya nodded firmly. "I'm right here with you," she said.

Boubou carefully tried the door handle, which was stuck at first. Then suddenly, with a loud clang that echoed off the walls, the handle gave way, and the door swung open. The noise seemed super loud to Boubou and Aya in the quiet cave.

They paused at the doorway, worried about what might be inside. Had someone heard them come in? Were smugglers hiding in the dark, ready to jump out? For several tense minutes, they stood still, listening hard for any sign of movement or sound.

As the silence continued, they realized the room was empty. Boubou turned on the flashlight, its beam cutting through the darkness, revealing the room's secrets.

They saw a big cave carved into the middle of the cliff, a natural cavern turned into a hidden hideout. The ceiling was held up by big beams, the sides were neatly cut, and the floor was smoothed out. This hidden room was a smuggler's secret place.

The flashlight showed huge crates, bundles, and packages scattered across the floor and stacked against the walls. A treasure trove of illegal goods.

"Smuggled stuff!" Boubou whispered, sounding amazed. "I can't believe it!"

"Looks like we've hit the jackpot. Not just diamonds, but all kinds of things," Aya said, sounding excited and shocked. "Look at all these boxes with foreign labels and military symbols."

"These must be worth a fortune," Boubou said, running his fingers over a crate labeled with unfamiliar characters.

Realizing they were alone in the room, Boubou and Aya went further inside, their flashlight lighting up every dark corner of the cave.

They started to explore the room more carefully. Among the mysterious crates of military equipment, they noticed expensive fabrics—rolls of silk and carelessly thrown tapestries worth a lot of money.

"This must be their main storage place," Aya said, looking closely at a crate. "There's got to be another way out of here, going up to the top of the cliff. They probably take everything up to Kambossa's place before shipping it out."

"But why wouldn't they just keep all this at the house?" Boubou wondered out loud.

"Maybe they're worried about the house getting searched. It's almost impossible to find here unless you know exactly where to look," Aya guessed. "And look at how well-hidden the entrance is."

Boubou looked around the room. "But how do they move all this stuff? I don't see any other exits."

Aya frowned, thinking hard. "There has to be a way. They can't possibly haul everything back through that narrow path we came from."

The flashlight beam moved across the walls, looking for any hint of a passage or door. But all they saw were the solid rock walls of the cave—no doorway, no exit, just the stone walls of their secret find.

"You're right. There's got to be another way out," Boubou insisted, frustration creeping into his voice.

"Maybe there's a hidden mechanism or a camouflaged door," Aya suggested. She started tapping on the walls, listening for any hollow sounds. "Help me look. There has to be something we're missing."

Boubou joined her, feeling along the seams and edges of the walls.

They worked together, carefully inspecting every inch of the cavern, determined to uncover the secrets of the smugglers' hideout.

In one corner, a stack of boxes caught their attention. Boubou accidentally bumped his flashlight against one, making a hollow sound.

"It's empty," he realized out loud.

A sudden thought hit him. Could these boxes be cleverly placed to hide a secret exit? He told Aya what he was thinking.

"But how could they stack these up after leaving?" Aya asked, wondering about the idea.

Boubou wasn't giving up. "This gang's smart enough to figure it out. Let's see what's behind these boxes."

He reached for the top box. It was surprisingly light, and he easily lifted it off the pile.

"I knew it!" Boubou exclaimed, sounding triumphant as he showed what was behind the stack.

The flashlight beam revealed the top part of a door, hidden behind the boxes. Quickly and excitedly, they cleared the boxes away, showing the whole door. Then, they understood the clever trick the smugglers had used.

The door had a small wooden platform attached to its bottom, sticking out over the cave floor. This platform was where the boxes were always kept. Boubou figured out, "They're always kept there as a trick. When someone goes out and shuts the door, the boxes on the platform swing in, making it look like they're just stacked on the floor."

This clever trick made the siblings grudgingly respect how smart the smugglers were.

"What now?" Aya asked, peering into the dark space beyond the door. "Do we keep going?"

Boubou nodded, looking determined. "We've already come this far. There's no point in turning back now. Let's see where this leads." With that, they got ready to step through the doorway, going further into the unknown parts of the smugglers' hideout.

Boubou stepped forward with the flashlight, showing a new set of stairs leading from the rocky landing. But he stopped suddenly, his hand grabbing Aya's arm in a silent warning.

"Voices," he whispered urgently.

They both froze, listening hard. A man's voice echoed faintly in the distance. Although they couldn't make out the words, the voices and the unmistakable sound of footsteps were getting closer.

In a quick, silent agreement, they returned to the secret room.

"Quick, the door," Boubou whispered.

They gently shut the door, moving as quietly as they could.

"Now, the boxes. They'll know someone's been here if they see them moved. Hurry."

Frantically but still trying to be silent, Boubou and Aya put the boxes back on the wooden platform attached to the door. Their hearts were pounding as the footsteps got louder, coming closer and closer to their hiding place.

Finally, with a quiet sense of relief, they placed the last box on top of the pile, fixing the clever disguise just as the footsteps seemed right outside.

In a rush of panic, they ran across the room towards the door leading back to the stairs leading down to the water. But just as they got close, they heard the unmistakable sound of the latch rattling on the opposite side of the cave.

"Too late," Boubou breathed out, his voice barely a whisper. "Hide."

The flashlight quickly scanned the area, showing several boxes nearby, covered with a heavy roll of silk. The fabric's folds fell to the floor, creating a perfect hiding spot. Without hesitating, they squeezed behind the boxes, pressing tightly against the wall, holding their breath in suspense.

They had barely hidden themselves and turned off the flashlight when they heard the other door creaking open. The tension was high as they waited in the dark, hoping their quick hiding spot would keep them from being found.

Boubou and Aya's hearts raced as they overheard the conversation, every word making them more nervous in their cramped hiding spot.

"We need to get that crate of rough rocks upstairs," the deep voice continued. "Bakana says he's got a buyer ready. No point in keeping it here."

"Got it," replied another voice. "Is there anything else we need to move?"

"Not right now. We're waiting to move the rest until the end of the week. It's too risky at the moment. Let Bakana handle his current load, including this batch, and then we'll take a break for a bit. I've got a bad feeling."

"And the boss?" asked the first voice, curious about what the leader thought.

"That's his plan too. Hang on, let me turn on the lights."

With a soft click, the entire room was suddenly filled with electric light. Boubou and Aya stayed completely still, hidden behind the boxes and silk, as their hearts pounded loudly in their ears.

The footsteps approached their hiding spot, each step echoing ominously in the cave.

＊　＊　＊

CHAPTER SIXTEEN

Threats And Ultimatums

Boubou and Aya were super tense, knowing how much danger they were in. The bright electric light hanging from the middle of the ceiling made everything so clear that they were sure they'd be seen. The boxes they were hiding behind had gaps between them. They would have been easy to spot if it weren't for the silk fabric draped over the opening.

"Hey, what about the silk?" one of the men said. "Maybe I should take it up, too. Bakana said it's going to the sweatshops soon."

Boubou's heart sank. "We're done for," he thought desperately. "If he gets close enough to grab that silk, he'll see us for sure."

But his partner didn't seem to want to do extra work. "Why bother? You won't get a pat on the back for carrying all that stuff upstairs. Even if Bakana plans to ship it out soon. And if he doesn't, you'll have to bring it back down. In this gang, I only do what Scorpion says—nothing more, nothing less."

"You've got a point. Let's just stick to the stones."

To Boubou and Aya's immense relief, the man turned away and returned to the room's far side. They heard a faint rustling noise. Then they heard, "Alright, that's everything. Time to head back up."

With a click, the cave went dark again. It was a welcome cover for the two kids, hidden behind their thin hiding spot. They finally let themselves breathe normally. They heard the door shut softly, followed by the men's footsteps going up the stairs in the passageway, getting fainter and fainter.

Once the sound of footsteps was gone, Boubou turned on the flashlight, letting out a big breath he didn't know he was holding.

"That was way too close," he whispered, his voice shaky. "I thought for sure we were going to get caught."

"We wouldn't have had a chance against those guys," Aya said quietly and seriously. "I bet they had guns."

"Did you hear what they said?" Boubou asked, his tone changing. "They're running sweatshops. Here in Africa, can you believe it?"

"Great, add child labor to their list of crimes," Aya growled. "And those military boxes, they're full of rocks? Just 'rough rocks,' they said. What's that about?"

Boubou nodded thoughtfully. "Let's look inside one of these boxes."

They went over to a heavy military box. Using a crowbar leaning against one of the boxes, they carefully opened it, trying not to make any noise. Inside, they found a bunch of uncut, rough diamonds glinting dully in the flashlight's beam.

"I think 'rough rocks' is a code name for blood diamonds," Boubou said gravely.

"So, what do we do now?" Aya asked, looking at her brother.

"We follow them," Boubou decided firmly.

"I'm in," Aya agreed with a nod. "We're definitely onto something big."

They closed the box again, making it look like no one had touched it.

"And let's not forget we might walk right into a bunch of smugglers if we're not careful. Things are about to get even trickier," Boubou warned.

"It can't be more scary than it's already been. I feel like I aged ten years while those guys were in here," Aya joked, trying to lighten the mood.

Quietly, they walked across the room and opened the door again, ready to face whatever was ahead.

Carefully, going once more through the hidden door behind the stacked boxes, Boubou and Aya stepped onto the landing, softly closing the door behind them. The staircase stood in front of them, steep and scary.

"I'll go first," Boubou whispered very quietly. "Stay right behind me."

He decided to turn off the flashlight. There was a slight chance that the smugglers might have left someone to watch at the top. If so, any light would show that they were there. So, in total darkness, they started climbing up, each step taken as quietly as possible.

They reached the top of the first set of stairs, finding themselves on a small platform. It was just planks laid against the rocky wall, stretching for quite a distance before leading to another set of wooden stairs.

They stopped and listened hard. It was hushed, with only the distant sound of waves hitting the cliff.

"I can't hear anything," Aya whispered, sounding nervous.

"Let's keep going," Boubou replied, sounding determined.

The passage through the rock was deep, and they kept going up, climbing what felt like endless stairs. Their legs started to get tired. They had never really realized how tall the cliff was—until now.

Finally, their long climb brought them to what seemed to be the last landing, where they found another door. This last door was mysterious: it could open to the outside, or it could lead into an underground cave just below the ground, or, as Boubou thought, it might even connect to the basement of Kambossa's house.

Boubou and Aya pressed themselves against the door, moving as quietly as shadows at night. They listened hard, trying to hear any sound of people on the other side.

It was completely silent.

Remembering how close they came to getting caught earlier, they decided to wait a little longer before going forward. This turned out to be a smart choice.

The kids stayed still, listening for the tiniest sound. At first, everything was quiet on the other side of the door, giving no clue about what was ahead. But after a tense five minutes, they heard a strange shuffling noise, followed by a soft sigh.

"Someone's there," Boubou whispered, barely audible.

Aya nodded silently in the dark.

They weren't sure what to do. It seemed like someone was on the other side—maybe a guard. They thought about trying to overpower this one person. Still, they were worried about making noise and alerting the rest of the smugglers.

But their problem was suddenly solved for them.

A door slammed somewhere far away, followed by the muffled sound of voices and footsteps coming closer. The noise got louder and more precise.

"I'm telling you, this nonsense has gone on long enough. He'll sign, and he'll sign right now, or I'll take stronger action."

The kids looked at each other, recognizing the voice. It belonged to the man who had angrily chased them away from the cove earlier that day.

"That's right, boss!" another voice agreed. "Make him sign. Then he'll have no choice but to keep quiet."

"If he refuses, he won't live long enough to regret it," the first speaker said coldly.

Suddenly, a switch clicked, and a thin yellow beam of light came under the door, cutting through the darkness at the kids' feet. The sound of movement and voices showed that three or four men had come into the room next door.

"He's still here," the one called the boss said, his voice sounding like he was in charge as he moved across the room. The kids heard the sound of a chair scraping against the floor. "You'll find it's much easier to get into this place than to leave it."

A tired, quiet voice answered, but it was too faint for Boubou and Aya to hear the words.

"You're our prisoner," the boss continued, his voice hard and mean. "And you'll stay that way until you die unless you sign that paper."

The air outside the door felt tense as the smugglers' threats worsened.

"You won't sign, huh? We'll see about that!" the leader's voice threatened.

"Just wait until he's been hungry for a few days. Then he'll change his mind," another man said, followed by rough laughter from the others.

"Yeah, you'll be starving before we're done with you. That's a promise," the harsh voice kept going. "So, are you going to sign or not?"

"No," came the firm but tired answer from the prisoner.

Boubou and Aya pressed against the door and looked at each other in the dark. Who could this prisoner be, and what did he know about the smugglers that made him such a big threat to them? This question bothered both kids as they listened closely to the scary conversation.

"You know too much about what we do," the leader's voice got more threatening. "You've discovered too many of our secrets, and we can't let you leave here to use that information against us. Understand this clearly: you either sign that paper, or you starve."

The prisoner stayed silent, showing he was either brave or hopeless.

One of the smugglers, eager to do something, made a cruel suggestion. "How about we use a hot iron to convince him?"

But the leader said no, thinking practically. "No, that's too dangerous. Let's not forget who he is. I'm giving him a fair chance. He signs now, or he faces what happens next."

The prisoner stayed completely silent, not even answering the threats.

"Getting stubborn, huh? Can't even say a word back?" The leader's voice showed he was getting annoyed and running out of patience.

Suddenly, his voice got louder, sounding very threatening: "Sign this paper, Chief, or you'll starve to death—as sure as my name is Scorpion!"

145

* * *

CHAPTER SEVENTEEN

The Smuggler's Snare

Boubou and Aya held their breath while listening to the tense conversation through the door.

"I won't sign it," Chief Gaye said firmly, his voice unmistakable.

"Sign or starve," Scorpion snapped back, his tone chilling.

"I'll starve then," Chief Gaye replied without hesitation.

Scorpion's voice turned mocking. "You might be hungry now, Gaye, but just wait. Your hunger and thirst will become unbearable. Soon, you'll do anything for a crumb or a sip of water."

But Chief Gaye didn't budge. "I won't sign."

Scorpion tried a different approach. "Look, we're not asking much. You stumbled onto things we'd rather you forget. Just go home to Zinguichou and pretend you never found out about us. No one even knows you're here."

"I've learned more about you and your operations than I ever wanted to, Scorpion," Chief Gaye replied, his voice heavy with determination. "I've got enough evidence to put you in jail for life. And that's not all."

"What do you mean—'not all'?" Scorpion asked, sounding worried.

"I know about the kids working in your sweatshops," Chief Gaye said bluntly.

The room erupted in angry shouts, with several smugglers yelling at once.

"You're out of your mind!" Scorpion yelled, but he sounded nervous. "That's nonsense. I don't know anything about sweatshops!"

"I have enough evidence to charge you with crimes against humanity," Chief Gaye insisted.

Scorpion's voice turned threatening. "That just gives us more reason to make sure you don't leave without signing. You're lucky we're even offering you a way out alive. If it were up to me, I'd just finish you off and throw you off the cliff into the sea."

"I won't sign," Chief Gaye repeated, his voice steady.

"Don't be a fool," Scorpion growled. "All we want is for you to admit you're part of our group. Then you can't turn us in without getting yourself in trouble too. You must realize you've learned some of our secrets, and we can't just let you go tell the authorities."

"So you trust me quite a bit, then?" Chief Gaye asked, sounding both defiant and curious. "What's to stop me from signing your paper and then going back on my word?"

"We understand you, Chief Gaye," one of the smugglers said confidently. "Once you sign, you'll be too scared of jail to talk."

Chief Gaye scoffed. "Scared? Me? Clearly, you don't know me at all. Have you forgotten about the Lighthouse diamond heist? I caught the most notorious diamond thief in Africa. I'm not afraid of anything. My reputation for bravery and integrity as Zinguichou's Chief of Police stands. I wouldn't be doing my job if I agreed to cover for you."

The smuggler tried a different angle. "What about your family? Your fellow officers? Aren't you being stubborn at their expense?"

There was a heavy silence. Then Chief Gaye spoke slowly but firmly. "They'd rather I die doing my duty than come back as a protector of smugglers and criminals."

"Such a high sense of duty," Scorpion sneered. "But hunger and thirst might change your mind. Are you thirsty?"

Chief Gaye said nothing.

"Are you hungry?"

Still no answer.

"You'll get hungrier and thirstier," Scorpion said. "We'll make it worse by putting food and water just out of your reach. You'll die slowly from thirst and starvation—unless you sign that document."

"As long as I'm breathing, I'll never sign it," Chief Gaye said firmly.

"Fine," Scorpion snapped. "Let's go, guys. We'll leave him alone to think about his situation."

Footsteps echoed as Scorpion and his men left the room. The sound faded until a door slammed shut, leaving Chief Gaye alone.

Aya, driven by a sudden urge, started toward the door, but Boubou quickly held her back. "Wait," he whispered urgently. "They might have left someone to watch him."

The siblings stood by the door, straining to hear any sounds. The room beyond remained silent. Finally sure Chief Gaye was alone, Boubou carefully reached for the door handle.

Moving slowly and quietly, he opened the door just a crack, enough to peek inside. His eyes adjusted to the dim light as he looked around.

Boubou scanned the cellar-like room he could now see. It was damp and musty, feeling neglected and hopeless. Unlike the cave-like storage room in the cliff, this space looked roughly dug out of the earth. Wooden planks made a makeshift floor, and a single light bulb cast a weak yellow glow. There was a simple table, a few chairs, and a small camp bed in one corner—a pretty dismal place.

Chief Gaye lay on that bed, a pitiful sight. He was tied up tightly, both hands and feet bound to the cot. The ropes were so tight he could barely move an inch. Lying flat on his back, he stared at the muddy ceiling, looking completely helpless. On a chair next to his cot was a large piece of paper—the contract the smugglers wanted him to sign.

Across the room, on a small table just out of Chief Gaye's reach, was a cruel trick by the smugglers. There sat a simple sandwich and a bottle of water. It wasn't much, but it must have looked like a feast to a starving man. This was clearly there to torture him, showing him food he couldn't have.

Chief Gaye didn't notice as Boubou opened the door. As Boubou watched him, he was shocked by how the Chief looked. The once strong man now seemed like a shadow of himself. He had lost a lot of weight; his face was thin, his cheeks hollow. He showed clear signs of insufficient food or water for a long time.

Seeing Chief Gaye like this made Boubou angry and sad. The situation was much worse than they thought, and they needed to act fast.

In the dim light, Boubou and Aya moved silently but quickly. They knew the smugglers could come back any second, and they had to hurry to save Chief Gaye.

When Chief Gaye heard a faint noise, he slowly turned his head. His eyes widened with surprise and relief when he saw the siblings carefully approaching. He almost gasped but managed to stay quiet, though his face showed a flash of hope.

Boubou rushed to his side and pulled out his pocket knife. He started working on the ropes tying up the Chief. But it was more complicated than he expected. The blade wasn't very sharp, and the ropes were thick and tough, resisting his attempts to cut them.

Aya looked around frantically for anything that could help but found nothing. She started trying to untie the stubborn knots with her hands.

Time was their enemy, and the threat of the smugglers coming back hung over them like a dark cloud. They worked as fast as possible while still being careful, racing against time.

Boubou struggled with the dull knife, barely making a dent in the thick ropes. Aya, determined to help, fought with the knots. Her fingernails cracked from the effort, but the ropes hardly budged.

Minutes crawled by, feeling like hours. Chief Gaye, still tied up and powerless, could only lie still. He couldn't even whisper encouragement. The only sounds were Boubou and Aya's quick breathing and the faint scraping of the knife against the ropes.

Finally, Boubou's knife cut through one of the ropes. Chief Gaye's feet were free at last! Boubou quickly pulled off the ropes, but a loose end hit the floor with a soft thud. In the quiet room, it sounded huge to the nervous siblings.

With renewed urgency, Boubou started on the ropes around Chief Gaye's arms. But just as he got the knife in position, a chilling sound cut through the tense atmosphere, sending a jolt of fear through Boubou and Aya.

Footsteps echoed ominously, a stark reminder of their dangerous situation. The smugglers were coming back to the underground room. Time was running out.

Boubou worked frantically with the knife, his efforts finally paying off as the rope began to loosen. With a considerable effort, Chief Gaye strained against his bindings, and with a final snap, the rope gave way. He was free, but their relief was short-lived.

The sound of several smugglers' footsteps coming down the stairwell grew louder.

"Quick!" Boubou urged in a hushed voice, tossing the ropes aside.

But Chief Gaye was struggling. "I-I can't hurry," he gasped, his voice weak. The long confinement had taken its toll, and his exhaustion was evident. "I've been here too long."

"We have to move, Chief!" Boubou pleaded, his voice filled with urgency. "Try to make it!"

The Chief, summoning the little strength he had left in him, replied, "I'll-I'll do my best."

Aya, sensing the imminent danger, spoke with a mix of fear and determination. "If those guys come back, we'll have to fight."

"You bet we'll fight," Boubou responded, his voice resolute.

As Chief Gaye staggered to his feet, the impact of his long captivity was obvious. He swayed unsteadily, almost falling before Aya quickly steadied him. The effects of being tied up for so long, along with hunger, had left him weak and disoriented, but he quickly tried to gather his wits.

Boubou and Aya moved quickly towards the door they had come through. Meanwhile, Chief Gaye stumbled to the table where the sandwich lay unattended. With a swift motion, he grabbed it. Taking a large, hasty bite, the Chief savored the taste of victory—a simple sandwich never tasted so good. But his triumph was brief as he realized he needed to catch up with Boubou and Aya. He made his way towards the door, his steps unsteady, still recovering from the numbness in his limbs from being tied up so long.

However, their hope of sneaking out was quickly dashed. The unmistakable sound of the smugglers' rough voices was alarmingly close, just outside the other door. Escape seemed impossible.

The opposite door burst open as the Diouf siblings and Chief Gaye reached the doorway. In the moment's chaos, Boubou caught a glimpse of Scorpion, the menacing figure from the cove, flanked by a group of tough-looking men. The situation escalated rapidly as Scorpion, with a swift, practiced motion, pulled a revolver from his pocket.

Scorpion, though surprised by the unexpected presence of the Diouf siblings and Chief Gaye, quickly regained his composure. His actions were fast and precise. The gun was aimed at Boubou in an instant, even before he could react to shut the door.

Without a word, Scorpion pulled the trigger. The sound of the gunshot was deafening in the small space, its echo bouncing off the walls. The bullet struck the door, sending splinters of wood flying.

Boubou, reacting on instinct, ducked out of the line of fire. Aya, who was ahead of him, quickly dodged to the side. Still weakened and unsteady, Chief Gaye managed to stumble out onto the landing at the top of the stairs.

Scorpion, fueled by rage and determination, shouted after them. "Come back!" he bellowed, charging across the room. "Come back, or I'll fire again!"

The situation had escalated to a dangerous climax. They were in immediate danger, not only from Scorpion's anger but also from the threat of more gunfire. The need to escape was now a matter of life and death.

Boubou's sudden and daring attack caught Scorpion off-guard. With a swift, crouching leap, he lunged at the smuggler leader. His strike was precise, hitting Scorpion's wrist and sending the revolver clattering across the floor, sliding into a corner.

They clashed in a fierce grapple, Boubou's element of surprise sending Scorpion staggering against the wall. However, this moment of advantage was short-lived. Scorpion's accomplices quickly intervened, rushing to his aid. Despite his bravery and quick thinking, Boubou was soon overpowered by the numbers against him and forcefully pulled away from the fight.

Meanwhile, the other smugglers, their revolvers drawn, chased Aya and Chief Gaye onto the landing. The threat of gunfire left them with no choice but to surrender. They were unarmed and stood no chance against the armed men who would shoot without hesitation.

The confrontation was brief but intense. The smugglers, with their threatening firearms, quickly gained the upper hand. The situation rapidly fell apart, with Chief Gaye once again bound to the cot and the Diouf siblings tied up and seated helplessly on chairs. In just minutes, they had all become captives at the mercy of the ruthless smuggling gang.

CHAPTER EIGHTEEN

Tangled In Treachery

SCORPION SHOOK OFF HIS SURPRISE AND SUDDENLY GRINNED. "Perfect timing!" he exclaimed. "Any later, and we would've missed our chance."

Aya and Boubou Diouf looked at each other, feeling defeated. Just moments ago, they'd almost escaped. Now, they were in even bigger trouble than before.

"What're we doing with them, boss?" one of the henchmen asked.

Aya and Boubou recognized the voice. They looked up and saw Greybeard, the same guy they'd run into at Kambossa's store. The day Boubou had found the Chief's hat.

"Well, that's tricky," Scorpion said, thinking. "We've got three prisoners now, not just one. Three people to keep quiet, three to watch."

Greybeard spoke up stubbornly. "We should've done what I said from the start. As long as Chief Gaye's alive, he's dangerous."

"You mean we should… get rid of him?" Scorpion asked.

"Exactly. And those nosy kids, too," Greybeard insisted.

Scorpion looked darkly at Chief Gaye on the cot. "Easier said than done," he muttered, but he sounded mean.

"Scorpion, haven't you done enough bad things already?" Chief Gaye said dramatically, sweating. "But I guess someone like you doesn't care about that," he added bitterly, sounding extra righteous. Though worried, he was thinking more about saving himself than Boubou and Aya.

"Don't worry about my conscience," Scorpion sneered, looking unsure. "What do you think you know about me, anyway?" he challenged angrily.

"Oh, I know plenty," Chief Gaye shot back. "Like how you took over Kambossa's treasure in that cliff house. And turned it into your smuggling hideout."

"Enough!" Scorpion snapped. "I'll deal with you and your little detectives soon enough; just wait."

Four of Scorpion's men were whispering at the back of the dim room. One big guy with a severe face stepped forward.

"Boss, we need to talk," he said to Scorpion.

Scorpion grumbled, "What now?"

The man hesitated, then pulled Scorpion away from the prisoners. "It's about those three we caught," he said carefully. "We know your business is your business, and we're not asking about Kambossa. But we're smugglers, not killers."

"That's right," another man agreed.

Scorpion laughed at them. "Getting scared?" he mocked. "Watch it, or I'll find a new crew!"

But the first man stood firm. "No, you won't," he said confidently. "We've been in this smuggling business with you from the start, and we expect our share of the money."

Another voice joined in. "We've got a different idea for the prisoners," he suggested. "It's a good plan."

Scorpion, curious, asked, "What plan?"

The talk shifted as one man said, "We've been thinking about Colonel Parker."

Scorpion asked, "What about him?"

"Give them to Colonel Parker. He's sailing to South Africa tomorrow morning. We could sneak them onto his ship," the man suggested.

Scorpion paused, thinking it over. He seemed to like the idea.

"Not bad," he mumbled. "I hadn't thought of Colonel Parker. He's perfect for this. He'll make sure they never come back," he said, smiling grimly.

Greybeard added meanly, "Colonel Parker might throw them overboard before they even see South Africa. He doesn't like wasting food on unwanted passengers. He'd rather feed the sharks if you know what I mean."

Scorpion nodded. "Even better. That way, our hands stay clean."

"Colonel Parker will handle it," the smuggler said confidently. "An old soldier like him would love to boss around three prisoners. He'll take care of them properly."

Scorpion picked up a paper from the floor that had fallen during the fight. He looked at it briefly, then tore it up. "We don't need this anymore. You missed your chance, Gaye. If you'd signed this, you could've gone free. But now, it's impossible. With three of you knowing about our business, it's too risky. You'll all go to Colonel Parker. He just brought in a shipment, and his ship leaves in the morning. You'll be part of his cargo!"

Chief Gaye stayed quiet, trying hard not to beg for his life.

Scorpion, looking for a reaction, asked, "Well? Nothing to say?"

Gaye answered sadly, "Do what you want with me. But leave the kids out of this."

Boubou quickly said, "We're staying with you, Chief."

"And that's a promise!" Aya added firmly.

Scorpion said finally, "You'll definitely all stay together. I can't risk any of you going back to Zinguichou to tell our secrets."

He stood in the middle of the room, smiling coldly as he looked at his prisoners. After a moment, he turned sharply to talk to his crew.

"They're tied up for now," he told Greybeard. "But we've got important business with Bakana. You two," he pointed at a couple of his men, "go down to the cove and row out. Signal Colonel Parker; we need the motorboat right away. The rest of you, come with me to load Bakana's truck. We can't have any nosy cops finding it in the lane."

Looking at the prisoners, Greybeard asked, "What about them?"

"They're not going anywhere," Scorpion assured him. "But just to be safe, we'll leave a guard. Momba, you stay here and watch them."

Momba, a tough-looking guy in overalls and a torn sweater, grunted and sat on a wooden box near the door. This seemed good enough for Scorpion, who left the room after warning Momba to keep his eyes open and make sure the prisoners didn't escape. Greybeard and the rest of the gang followed, except for a couple who went out a different way. Their boots echoed down the stairs, fading away below the cliff.

The room got very quiet after the smugglers left. Momba slouched over, looking grumpy and staring at the floor. A revolver stuck out of his hip pocket, looking dangerous.

Boubou twisted and turned, trying to get free from the ropes tying him to the chair. But those smugglers knew how to tie knots; he couldn't move more than an inch.

"I think we're in big trouble," Aya said quietly, sounding defeated.

Boubou was usually optimistic, but in this case, he couldn't see any hope in this horrible situation.

"I think you're right. Looks like we're going to meet Colonel Parker by morning," Boubou replied, worried.

"But Boubou, we don't want to go to South Africa," Aya protested, scared and confused.

"We might not even get to South Africa, Aya. Remember what those guys were saying? That creepy Colonel might just throw us into the ocean somewhere," Boubou said, trying to figure out their scary situation.

"Hey, shut up!" Momba suddenly yelled, his voice rough. "Be quiet, or things are gonna get real bad for you two," he warned, tapping his gun meaningly.

After Momba's threat, the room got quiet again. Boubou and Aya looked at each other, feeling scared and hopeless. There was no way out of this mess.

157

CHAPTER NINETEEN

The Daring Getaway

Chief Gaye glanced at Boubou and Aya, tied to their chairs. He was surprised to see Boubou smiling despite their scary situation. The Chief was about to ask why, but Boubou gave him a quick look that said, "Be quiet." Then, the Chief noticed the guard.

Momba wasn't watching them closely. He wasn't even looking their way. Instead, his head kept drooping like he was about to fall asleep.

Scorpion hadn't picked a very clever guard. Momba had been up all night helping with the smuggling from Colonel Parker's ship and hadn't slept since. He was super tired.

A few times, Momba jerked awake, rubbing his eyes to stay awake. But his head would always droop again, and he'd take little naps.

Meanwhile, Boubou had a plan. He remembered a trick his dad taught him when he was little. Magicians and escape artists used it to get out of ropes and even strait-jackets. When the smugglers were tying him up, Boubou had puffed up his chest and tensed his muscles as much as he could, keeping his arms away from his body. So when he relaxed, the ropes weren't as tight as the smugglers thought.

This gave Boubou a little room to move. He noticed the ropes around his right wrist were quite loose, so he started trying to get free. For a long time, it seemed hopeless, and the rope hurt his wrist. But finally, he managed to wiggle his hand out.

Aya and Chief Gaye watched with big eyes, looking hopeful as they saw Boubou quietly reaching for one of the knots. It was hard work, especially with just one free hand. The smugglers had tied the knot quickly and not very well, so after some struggling, Boubou loosened it enough that the rope ends came undone.

With his arms free, Boubou focused on freeing his feet. Luckily, they weren't tied as well as his hands, just with one loop of rope around each leg. After a few minutes of quiet, hard work, he slipped his feet out of the ropes.

Next, he removed his shoes and put them softly on the floor to stay quiet. Like a cat, Boubou stood up from his chair and started sneaking towards the guard.

Momba was half-asleep but not totally out of it. When Boubou had moved about six feet, a quiet creak from the floor woke Momba up. He turned, blinking in confusion and sleepiness.

Momba looked totally surprised when he saw Boubou. He opened his mouth to yell for help, but Boubou didn't give him the chance. He jumped on the smuggler in a flash, stopping Momba's shout to just a muffled grunt.

Boubou and Momba fought hard but quickly. As Momba tried to pull his gun from his pocket, Boubou pushed his knee harder against the man. This made Momba loosen his grip, letting out a pained groan. Boubou grabbed the gun and stepped back, pointing it at Momba.

"Don't make a sound," Boubou whispered.

Realizing he'd lost, Momba raised his hands in surrender, quiet and shocked. He sat on the floor, breathing hard, looking hurt and surprised.

Boubou saw a knife on Momba's belt and grabbed it. Keeping the gun pointed at Momba, he carefully stepped backward towards Aya.

He never took his eyes off Momba as he bent down and started cutting the ropes tying up his sister.

The knife easily cut through the ropes, and they fell away fast. Aya jumped up from her chair, shaking off the last bits of rope, and took the knife from Boubou. While her brother kept Momba under control with the gun, she hurried over to free Chief Gaye.

Boubou, still quiet and focused, pointed at the bed and told Momba to lie down on it. At first, Momba looked like he might not do it, but when Boubou jabbed the gun at him, he quickly changed his mind and obeyed.

Luckily, the ropes on the bed were still there, perfect for tying up Momba. Boubou and Aya worked fast and well, tying up the smuggler to the bed just like Chief Gaye minutes before. They even made a gag using Momba's own handkerchief and some of the rope from the chairs.

In less than five minutes, everything had changed completely. Their former captor was now the prisoner, lying on the bed, tightly tied up and gagged. His attempts to make noise were useless, just quiet, muffled grumbles.

Breaking the silence, Chief Gaye whispered, "What now?"

"We can't go out by the cove," Boubou said urgently. "There are a couple of guys down there, signaling to a motorboat. We should probably go upstairs."

"Upstairs? Where does that go?" asked Aya.

"Outside. It'll take us to a shed near the house," Chief Gaye explained.

Boubou moved towards the door, looking determined. "We need to hurry," he said. "I've got the gun with me. Just in case we run into someone—"

He slowly opened the door, peeking out carefully. Outside was just a stairway going up into the darkness.

With a silent nod, Boubou stepped forward, with Aya and the Chief right behind him. They went up the stairs, each step slow and careful. Aya had closed the door behind them, making it very dark, and Boubou didn't dare turn on the flashlight.

Finally, they reached the top. Boubou stopped, his hands feeling above him for something in the dark. As Aya and Chief Gaye watched, a small opening of grayish light slowly appeared above them, growing into a square. Against this light, they could see Boubou's head and shoulders. He had opened the hidden trapdoor that led out of the underground caves and tunnels.

Boubou looked out carefully, checking to see if any smugglers were around. There was no sign of them. He climbed to the top step and moved aside, making room for the others. Chief Gaye and Aya came out, looking like ghosts appearing from the ground. The three gathered under the shed, right behind the parked car.

The night was dark around them, with the baobab trees whispering in the wind from the sea. Kambossa's big house stood in front of them, hidden in shadows. Towards the lane, they could hear muffled noises—probably from the truck the smugglers were using to load stuff. These were probably the things they planned to sell through the man called Bakana.

"Looks like we're safe for now," Chief Gaye said quietly to Boubou and Aya.

They slipped out of the shed carefully, closing the trapdoor behind them. They stood together, blending into the shadows.

"We definitely can't take the lane," Boubou whispered, looking around.

"But we have to move," the Chief said softly. "We can come back for the prisoner later."

"Prisoner?" Boubou and Aya said in surprise.

"In the basement of that house," Chief Gaye explained quietly. "I heard them talking about someone being kept there."

Boubou frowned, looking worried. "I don't like leaving without freeing them."

"Maybe we should go into town, get some help," suggested the Chief, looking towards town.

"But if they realize we've escaped, they'll probably pack up and leave," Boubou pointed out.

"But we can't just take on this gang by ourselves. It's too dangerous, and we might all end up caught again," the Chief argued, sounding concerned.

Boubou thought for a moment. Then he sighed. "You're right; it's too risky. And I've already put Aya in too much danger. We should go back to town."

"I'm not some little kid, Boubou! Wherever you go, I'm going too!" Aya said fiercely.

Deciding to get help, they carefully walked across the grassy yard, heading for the bushes near the lane. The big, shadowy shape of the old stone house stood quietly in the night.

Then, suddenly, a loud noise broke the silence, scaring them all—the sound of the trapdoor being thrown open.

* * *

CHAPTER TWENTY

Cornered In The Shadows

S UDDENLY, A LOUD SHOUT BROKE THE QUIET NIGHT. "CHIEF! Greybeard! They've escaped. Look everywhere!"

The panicked voice came from someone climbing out of the shed, warning the other smugglers.

"Quick, to the house!" Boubou said sharply. He ran across the yard towards the big, dark building, with Chief Gaye and Aya tagging behind. The Chief kept trying to hold up his pants, which were too big now because he'd lost weight while captured.

The man from the shed saw them running. Suddenly, there were three bright red flashes and loud gunshots.

From the lane, they heard running footsteps and voices getting closer. "What's happening? What's going on?"

"They've escaped! Chief Gaye and the kids! They're running away. Look, they're going across the yard!"

More gunshots rang out. But the shots missed as Chief Gaye and the siblings quickly disappeared into the house's shadows.

With the noise getting louder behind them, they hurried towards the building. It was their only safe place. Going to the road would probably mean running into the smugglers, and going back through the tunnel would trap them at the cliff.

Boubou, leading the way, ran to the back door and opened it. The three rushed into the kitchen, quickly closing the door behind them.

Out of the darkness, a scared voice asked, "Who's there?"

The sudden voice startled them. They stayed quiet.

"Who's there, I said? Is it you, Greybeard?"

They still didn't answer. Boubou carefully moved through the dark towards the voice.

"Talk! Now! Talk, or I'll shoot!"

The Chief and Aya were surprised by a sudden scuffle. Boubou had jumped at the man in the dark. Chief Gaye and Aya didn't wait; they joined in the fight with the two wrestling figures.

Suddenly, there was a huge blast and flash of light. The homeowner, who had a shotgun, had accidentally fired it during the fight.

Luckily, Chief Gaye and Aya weren't hit. But the loud gunshot got the attention of the smugglers outside. In seconds, the back door burst open.

"They're in here!" someone yelled. "They've broken into the house!"

Boubou quickly pushed away the man he was fighting. "Upstairs!" he shouted to Chief Gaye and Aya, leading the way as he ran into the next room.

A small candle was burning at the bottom of the stairs. As they ran up, Aya quickly blew out the candle, darkening the room just as the first smuggler came through the door.

Boubou stopped at the top of the stairs, making sure Chief Gaye and Aya were beside him.

Downstairs, someone lit a match. Boubou quickly aimed and shot towards the small light. There was a surprised grunt as the smuggler soon put out the light, realizing his mistake in showing where he was. The smugglers whispered to each other.

"He's at the top of the stairs," one said quietly. "We can't just run up. The kid has a gun."

"Only one of them?"

"Yeah. The others don't have weapons."

"Let's wait until he's out of bullets. Then we'll get them."

The smugglers seemed to move back towards the kitchen door. Then, suddenly, there was a lot of gunfire.

But Boubou, Aya, and Chief Gaye had already moved around the corner of the stairs, safe from the bullets. They heard the shots hitting the stairs, but they weren't hurt.

"That should do it!" they heard Scorpion yell. "If they were on those stairs, they're done now."

"We should still be careful," another smuggler said. "The kid has a gun."

"Where'd he get that?"

"He took it from the guard," someone answered. "They had him tied up tight."

"Good thing we caught them before they totally escaped. Momba's gonna be in trouble!"

"They had the guard tied to the bed when we got there," another voice said. "Took his gun, gagged him. He said they'd just left, so we followed them, coming up through the trapdoor. Saw them as they were leaving the shed."

"If they'd made it to the woods, we'd have had a big chase. But now, they're trapped for sure."

In the quiet, the trio could hear even the softest whispers. Then, they heard something important: "The back stairs—"

Boubou quickly turned to Aya and Chief Gaye. "They're planning to come up the back stairs!"

Aya thought for a moment. "Didn't think of that," she said quietly. "Is there a way to get to the attic?"

Boubou turned on his flashlight. A few feet away, he saw another set of stairs going up to a trapdoor in the ceiling. At the same time, he heard soft noises at the bottom of a different set of stairs coming from the kitchen.

"Quick, this way!" he whispered urgently. They crept down the hall, reaching the stairs to the attic.

Chief Gaye went up first, with Aya right behind him, using the flashlight. Boubou stayed at the bottom, ready to use his gun to protect them if needed.

When Chief Gaye reached the attic trapdoor, he pushed hard against it, but the door wouldn't open. He pushed harder, but it still wouldn't move. To make things worse, Chief Gaye was also trying to keep his pants from falling down.

From below, Boubou called up, worried, "What's happening up there?"

"It's stuck," Aya called back, sounding scared.

"I'm having some pants problems here," Chief Gaye said, frustrated and embarrassed.

Hearing this, Boubou quickly climbed the rest of the stairs and joined in pushing. With both of them pushing, the trapdoor finally opened with a loud crash.

Instantly, a shout came from the stairs below. "Hurry, guys! They're getting into the attic!"

They heard heavy footsteps in the hallway as the smugglers ran up the stairs after them. Aya went through the opening first, followed by Chief Gaye. Boubou was only halfway there when the smugglers burst into the hallway. Without hesitating, the teenager aimed and fired.

The lead smugglers stumbled backward, trying to find cover, and crashed into their friends. There was chaos. Boubou took his chance, jumped up the last steps, squeezed through the small gap, and quickly slammed the trapdoor shut.

In total darkness, the Dioufs found themselves in an attic. Aya turned on a flashlight, showing a room full of old boxes and forgotten stuff under the roof. Dust floated in the light.

From below, they heard muffled voices. "Where did they go?" one of the smugglers called out, sounding frustrated.

"Up into the attic," another answered, sounding pleased. "Now they're trapped right where we want them."

In this small, dusty hiding place, the Dioufs huddled together, breathing fast and hearts pounding, ready for what would happen next.

"That's what you said last time," one of the smugglers said, not believing it.

"No way out this time. They're really trapped now," another said confidently.

Then, over all the talking, Scorpion's sharp and commanding voice came. "Chief Gaye!" he yelled.

Chief Gaye didn't answer.

"Listen up, Gaye!" Scorpion yelled louder. "You've got one minute to come down from there."

Still, no one answered.

"The floors aren't bulletproof, Chief!" Scorpion warned, sounding mean. "We can shoot right through them. You're trapped. It's better if you just come down."

In the attic, Boubou's flashlight moved around quickly, showing how bad their situation was. The smuggler was right; there was no way out. They really were trapped.

There was a tense silence, broken only by their nervous breathing. Then Scorpion's voice came again, more urgent this time. "This is your last chance, Chief!"

Aya's flashlight shone on Boubou, who was looking at his gun with a sad face. The gun was empty; no more bullets left.

"Boubou, you should've given me that gun from the start. This isn't a toy for young boys. I've got years of experience with these things," Chief Gaye said. "Now I'm here, so stop trying to be the hero, okay? Let me handle the shooting."

Suddenly, a gunshot came from below. A bullet zipped through the floor, just missing the trio, and made a hole right between Chief Gaye's legs in his oversized pants. The Chief jumped up, eyes wide, looking down at his pants that now had a new hole. Another shot hit the trapdoor, making wood splinters fly.

The trio quickly moved back. They quietly pressed their backs against the sloped walls of the attic, getting as far as they could from the trapdoor.

More shots rang out, each bullet hitting dangerously close. The attic was very tense.

Then, Scorpion's voice came again. "What do you think now, Chief? You and the kids ready to give up?"

But they stayed quiet, knowing any noise might show where they were and bring more bullets. When they didn't answer, Scorpion talked to his men.

"Give 'em another round!" one of the smugglers yelled.

A bunch of revolver shots rang out, echoing in the space. During this, some smugglers found a long pole and started poking at the trapdoor. The Dioufs, surprised, couldn't react in time. With a loud bang, the trapdoor swung open, hitting the attic floor.

A hand holding a revolver came through the opening, followed by the smuggler's head and shoulders. He squinted into the dim attic, gun ready. Below, someone had turned on a hall light, making a dark outline of the smuggler.

"Get out here now!" he yelled, aiming his revolver right at Boubou's shadowy figure. "Move, or I'll shoot!"

There was nothing they could do. Feeling hopeless, Boubou moved towards the hole in the floor, with Aya and Chief Gaye, hands up, following behind. In a funny struggle, the Chief tried to hold up his big pants and keep his hands up at the same time. The smuggler carefully went back down the steps, gun still pointed at them, until he reached the bottom.

Coming down into the hallway, the Dioufs saw a scary sight—a bunch of guns pointed right at them. Scorpion stood in front, looking very pleased. Once again, they were prisoners.

✳ ✳ ✳

CHAPTER TWENTY ONE

The Final Showdown

SCORPION STRUTTED FORWARD, HIS FACE TWISTED INTO AN ugly sneer. "Well, well!" he mocked. "Thought you could slip away, huh?"

Boubou, Aya, and Chief Gaye stayed quiet. They'd been so close to escaping, but now the smugglers had caught them again.

"You really thought you could outsmart me," Scorpion bragged.

One of his goons asked, "What do we do with them, boss?"

"Back to the cave," Scorpion ordered. "We need to hand them over to Colonel Parker right away. And listen up—if they escape again, you'll be in big trouble. Watch them like hawks."

"Should we tie them up?" another smuggler asked.

"No rope, but it's fine," Scorpion said. "Just shoot anyone who tries to be clever. Got it?" He glared at Chief Gaye. "You hear that? Try to run, and it's game over."

The smugglers surrounded them, their eyes mean and their guns ready. Boubou's weapon, now useless, was in the bad guys' hands.

"Move!" Scorpion yelled. "Downstairs, now!"

He shoved Chief Gaye with his gun. Boubou, Aya, and the Chief trudged down the stairs, feeling miserable. A smuggler led the way, watching for any last escape attempts.

In the dark basement, they paused as the lead smuggler lit a match. The light bulb was busted from an earlier fight. Just as the match flared, they heard running footsteps from the kitchen, and the back door slammed shut.

Another smuggler burst in, out of breath and looking scared. The match made creepy shadows on his face.

"The police!" he gasped. "They're coming down the road!"

Chaos broke out. Everyone started yelling at once as the smugglers scrambled down the stairs. Scorpion grabbed the newcomer by his shirt.

"Police? What are you talking about?" he demanded, shocked and angry.

"They're on the road," the man panted. "Came in a car... they're almost here!"

Scorpion laughed. "Chill out! There are only two cops in this tiny town. We can take them easily."

"No, you don't get it! It's not just local cops—it's a whole task force! State troopers, federal agents... We're totally outnumbered!"

Scorpion let out a furious yell and shoved the man away. "To the cave, now!" he roared.

In the chaos, the match went out, and the room plunged into darkness. Boubou saw his chance. He jumped at the smuggler next to him, knocking the gun from his hand. It clattered to the floor with a loud bang.

"Help!" the smuggler yelled as they wrestled, his voice bouncing off the walls.

In the pitch-black room, Boubou relied on his other senses. He could feel the smuggler moving and hear him breathing. He dodged as the man lunged at him, barely missing.

Boubou fought back, throwing punches in the dark. His heart raced as he moved quickly, using the darkness to his advantage. The smuggler, without his gun and unable to see, swung wildly.

The fight was silent but intense. Boubou could feel the smuggler getting more frustrated with each missed punch. Suddenly, Boubou kicked low, hitting the smuggler's knee. He heard the man stumble and quickly twisted his arm behind his back.

Meanwhile, Aya sprang into action. She threw herself at Scorpion, knocking him down. In the darkness, they rolled around, fighting fiercely. Aya's fist found Scorpion's jaw, and he yelped in pain. Scorpion, not used to fighting someone so small and quick, struggled to defend himself.

The room was in total chaos, with everyone fighting their own battles in the dark.

Suddenly, the front door banged loudly. A booming voice shouted from outside, "Task force! The house is surrounded! Give up now— there's no way out!"

Scorpion, in a panic, broke free from Aya. He swung his fists wildly, sending Aya flying across the room. Then he dashed to the kitchen and yanked open the back door, desperate to escape.

But there, blocking his way, stood a task force officer with a gun pointed at him. Scorpion yelled a warning to his gang, "The cops are here! Run! Every man for himself!"

The officer fired, but Scorpion dodged the bullet. The other smugglers rushed into the kitchen, pushing past the officer and pinning him against the wall.

Everything was in total chaos. The house was dark, and outside, the night air filled with gunshots, shouts, and angry yells.

❖

One of the smugglers dashed to the shed, yanking open the trapdoor with sweaty hands. Just before disappearing down the steps, he yelled to his buddies, "To the boat, let's go!" His voice cut through the chaos, and several others followed him quickly, scrambling for freedom in the darkness.

Outside, about six task force officers swarmed the yard like angry bees. They'd heard the gunshots and planned to surround the house, hoping to trap the whole gang. Their plan might have worked if it wasn't for the lookout, who'd warned the others just in time.

Boubou was locked in a fierce wrestling match with a smuggler in the pitch-black living room. The guy was built like a tank and tough as nails, pushing Boubou to his limits. Each was driven by desperation: the smuggler feared getting caught, and Boubou had a burning determination not to let his opponent escape.

Meanwhile, Chief Gaye, totally overwhelmed by the craziness, stumbled towards the kitchen door. As he got closer, one of the remaining smugglers rushed past him like a bullet. The sudden movement made the Chief freeze up like a statue. Chief Gaye flattened himself against the door, hands up in surrender. In all the commotion, his pants slipped down to his ankles. The smuggler gave Chief Gaye a look that said, "You've got to be kidding me," and zipped out the door.

Back in the other part of the house, Aya was shaking off being thrown against a wall by Scorpion. She bounced back to her feet like a rubber ball, unfazed and ready for more. She immediately started chasing after Scorpion, following the direction he'd run. In the kitchen, it seemed Scorpion had bumped into a task force officer, forcing him to turn tail and look for another way out. Guided by the sound of Scorpion's hurried footsteps, Aya kept up the chase.

Scorpion burst into a front room and slammed the door behind him with a bang. Aya, not about to give up, threw herself against the locked door. With a mighty effort, she charged at it, shoulder first. The wood cracked under the impact like dry twigs. Another powerful thrust and the door gave way, sending her stumbling into the room.

But Scorpion had pulled a Houdini—he was gone.

The room, dimly lit by a wide window, revealed a dark patch on the floor—a trapdoor. Aya moved towards it, discovering a staircase leading down into what looked like a creepy basement. She descended, following the echo of fading footsteps in the gloom.

Pausing to listen, she could hear Scorpion's hurried steps moving further away. Then, surprisingly, a voice bounced off the walls. A faint glow of light appeared in the distance, like a firefly in the night. Aya realized the cellar was divided. Scorpion had entered a small room on the other side. She carefully moved towards the light, determined to discover what was happening.

Aya crept forward silently, her senses on high alert. The dimly lit room ahead echoed with voices—one mean and angry, the other trembling with fear.

"What's happening up there?" the scared voice asked.

Scorpion's response was bitter. "Everything's falling apart. Task force officers are swarming the place like ants at a picnic."

"Task force?" the voice quivered in disbelief.

"Yeah, the whole cavalry—government agents, local police, everyone. But don't think you'll get a chance to rat us out. I should've dealt with you ages ago."

The terror in the captive's voice shot up like a rocket. "No, Scorpion, please! I don't want to die!"

Aya, heart pounding, peeked into the doorway. She saw Scorpion standing over a small bed, where a man with handcuffs and messy hair cowered, his feet chained to the bed's leg. In Scorpion's hand was a heavy club, his face twisted in a cruel snarl that would scare a grizzly bear.

Without hesitating, Aya's eyes darted around the room and landed on a crate of empty bottles against the wall. She grabbed one, feeling its solid weight in her hand. With the bottle clutched tight, she charged into the room just as Scorpion was about to bring his club down. In one swift motion, she smashed the bottle against his head like she was swinging a baseball bat.

The surprise attack sent Scorpion reeling back against the wall, the club slipping from his hand as he grabbed his bleeding head. Dazed and confused, he fumbled for his gun, but Aya was quicker than a cat. She snatched up the fallen club and, with a surge of adrenaline, whacked Scorpion's hand. The gun went flying across the room like a frisbee.

Feeling brave and determined, Aya swung the club again, catching Scorpion on the head. The second hit knocked the dazed smuggler to the floor, ending the immediate danger.

But Scorpion wasn't ready to throw in the towel just yet. With a sudden burst of energy, he kicked out, shoving Aya so hard she tumbled back across the muddy floor. But Aya, tough as nails, scrambled to her feet in a flash. In one smooth move, she dove for Scorpion's revolver where it had fallen.

With the gun now pointed steadily at Scorpion's face, the tables turned faster than a flipped pancake. The hardened smuggler, realizing he was beaten, raised his hands in surrender.

"You win, girl," he admitted, his voice sour with defeat.

Keeping a firm grip on the revolver, Aya stood up carefully, her eyes never leaving Scorpion. The sounds of chaos still rang out from upstairs, where the police were wrestling with the remaining smugglers.

"Upstairs!" Aya commanded sharply, sounding like a seasoned Detective from a TV show. She then glanced quickly at the chained man on the cot. "We'll be back for you in a minute—Mr. Hounsou."

✳ ✳ ✳

CHAPTER TWENTY TWO

The Round-Up

Amid all the chaos, Boubou found himself right in the thick of things. He'd bravely tackled one of the smugglers in the living room, using a cool pinning move his dad had taught him. This was super important because it happened just as Aya was chasing Scorpion towards the secret trapdoor that led to an underground basement. Boubou's awesome dad-taught technique and his strength let him keep the smuggler pinned down just long enough for a task force officer to run in and slap handcuffs on the bad guy.

Catching his breath, Boubou realized that while three smugglers were now caught, thanks to the officers outside, just as many were still trying to escape. What's worse, none of the task force or police seemed to know about the secret trapdoor some smugglers had used to get away.

Boubou then bumped into Chief Gaye, who awkwardly pulled up his pants as he exited the kitchen. "You okay, Chief Gaye?" Boubou asked, concerned.

Still struggling with his rebellious pants, Chief Gaye puffed out his chest like a proud rooster. "Had myself a little scuffle with one of those smugglers. Showed him what the law's all about!" he boasted, throwing a few pretend punches in the air.

Boubou nodded, then suggested, "Maybe you should let the medics check you out. I need to tell the others about the trapdoor—it's super important they know."

Stepping outside, Boubou was hit by a whirlwind of activity. It was like being in the middle of a TV cop show: task force vehicles were parked everywhere, flashing red and blue lights. Officers were running around, looking busy and important. Some were handcuffing the caught smugglers and marching them to a big task force truck. Everyone was yelling orders and updates, creating a noisy symphony of law enforcement in action.

Boubou spotted an officer who had just handcuffed a smuggler and made a beeline for the shed. The car they'd been chasing earlier was still there, like a silent witness to all the craziness. "They escaped this way!" he yelled to the officer, his voice cutting through the noise like a knife.

The officer reacted instantly, calling for backup. Soon, a group of task force members followed Boubou to the trapdoor. As Boubou reached the edge, he saw a faint light below—the smugglers were still down there, trying to sneak away in the dark. The task force officer quickly gave orders to his team, and soon, footsteps echoed on the stairs as they raced down. Knowing the layout, Boubou led the charge, plunging into the shadowy stairwell after the fleeing criminals.

When Boubou got to the door of the room where Chief Gaye had been held captive, he braced himself for anything. But when he went in, the room was weirdly empty. It looked like someone had left in a big hurry: stuff was thrown all over, a chair was knocked over, and the far door was wide open.

"Secret passages, huh?" an officer said, sounding surprised and impressed as he came in behind Boubou. This showed how clever the smugglers were and how tricky this whole situation was.

Without missing a beat, Boubou led the group through the open door and down the stairs that wound towards the bottom of the cliff. The officer who had spoken earlier now took the lead in lighting their way, his flashlight beam cutting through the darkness like a lightsaber. Their footsteps echoed as they hurried down, creating a steady beat in the otherwise quiet space.

Finally, they reached the storage room at the bottom. The air felt thick and tense as Boubou and the officers got ready to face whatever— or whoever—might be hiding in the shadows.

But the smugglers were nowhere to be seen, like ghosts that had vanished into thin air. The room looked like a tornado had hit it. Judging by the military crates and packages scattered all over the floor, it seemed the smugglers had tried to grab whatever they could in their rush, probably the smaller, unpolished blood diamonds.

"You seem to know this place pretty well," said one of the task force members, giving Boubou a curious look as he confidently led them across the room to the opposite door and onto the landing.

"I've been here once before, came in this way," Boubou explained, his voice steady. "There's a hidden water cave under us. I bet they used a boat to escape," he added, sounding both sure and like he was making an educated guess.

Excited by Boubou's insider knowledge, the team picked up their pace, eager to find more clues in their chase after the bad guys.

They raced down the passageway until they reached the cave. Just as Boubou had guessed, the boat was gone.

"They've escaped," he said, sounding disappointed, while the task force members shined their flashlights around the rocky cave.

Suddenly, a shout echoed through the darkness.

"Can someone shine a light over here?" a voice called out.

Boubou's face lit up like a Christmas tree. "That's Pierre!" he exclaimed.

Then, cutting through the silence, they heard the hum of a motorboat. Grabbing a flashlight, Boubou dashed towards the cave's entrance, his footsteps bouncing off the walls.

They spotted the motorboat not far away. Pierre was at the wheel, trying to find the right way in.

"Over here!" Boubou yelled, waving the light. "Go to the right of the cave where it's deeper. A little more… perfect!"

They could hear voices coming from Pierre's boat.

"Who's with you?" Boubou asked, curious.

"More task force, guys. The rest are up on the road in a car," Pierre answered.

As the boat got closer, Boubou saw it was packed with task force officers. Behind it, they were towing a rowboat with the three sneaky smugglers they'd been chasing, all handcuffed and looking grumpy.

The boat smoothly pulled up next to the rocky edge. Three officers jumped out, their guns ready. They'd caught the smugglers trying to make a run for it in the rowboat.

Pierre noticed Boubou looking at his dad's boat, the Riviera, which now had a few bullet holes in it.

"Yeah, they put up a big fight," Pierre said, still sounding pumped up from the chase. "But we got them!" he added proudly. "We caught them just as they tried to sneak out of the cove."

"We've caught them all then!" Boubou shouted excitedly. "The task force burst into the house and grabbed the rest of the smugglers there."

Meanwhile, the task force members were escorting the newly caught smugglers up to the house, climbing the long staircase while their buddies closely watched them.

"We thought these guys had gotten away," Boubou said, watching the smugglers being led off.

"Almost, but not quite," Pierre replied. "They nearly vanished from the cove right in front of us."

"If they'd escaped, we'd have lost them for good," Boubou thought out loud. "They were headed for a ship."

"A ship?" An officer with sergeant stripes stepped forward, suddenly interested. "Did they say anything about a ship?"

"One of them, Colonel Parker, has a ship waiting outside the bay," Boubou shared, remembering what the smugglers had said.

"Awesome!" the Sergeant grinned. Now we can catch the whole gang." He turned to Pierre. "Do you think your boat can make another trip?"

"You bet, sir!" Pierre answered eagerly, ready to help.

The Sergeant then spoke to another officer. "We need as many officers as we can get for backup. We're going to find that ship. Colonel Parker, right?" he checked with Boubou.

"Yep, that's the name I heard," Boubou nodded.

The tall Sergeant, who looked important, turned back to Boubou and Pierre. He started explaining that he was the boss of a special international task force. Their job was to stop the smuggling, which was causing problems all along this part of the African coast.

"Listen up, boys," the Sergeant began, his voice firm but not unfriendly. "I lead an international task force focused on stopping smuggling operations along the African coast."

Pierre and Boubou's eyes widened with interest.

The Sergeant smiled. "What we're dealing with here is serious. It involves illegal trade in everything from blood diamonds and weapons to endangered wildlife. It's a serious issue that's affecting the entire region."

Pierre was eager to help. "So, how can we assist?"

"Colonel Parker, the guy we're after, isn't just smuggling blood diamonds. He's also running sweatshops all over Africa," the Sergeant began, sounding really upset. "Sweatshops are factories where people, often kids, are forced to work in terrible conditions. They hardly get paid anything, it's unsafe, and they have no rights. It's basically modern-day slavery," he explained, his words making the crimes sound even worse.

"These sweatshops take advantage of people who can't defend themselves, especially children who should be in school, not working in factories. They're made to work super long hours, often in dangerous places, using unsafe machines or chemicals without any protection. It ruins these kids' lives—hurting them physically, mentally, and emotionally. They don't get to go to school, have a normal childhood, or plan for their future," he continued, looking worried and determined to stop it.

"Creeps like Colonel Parker aren't just stealing diamonds; they're stealing kids' chances to be kids and have hope. That's why our task force is here—to stop these awful crimes and make sure people like Parker get punished," the Sergeant finished, his eyes showing how serious he was about it.

Everyone felt a new sense of urgency as the Sergeant's words sank in. Pierre nodded solemnly and turned the boat around, ready to go at any second. Looking angry but determined, Boubou stared out at the sea, preparing his mind for what was coming next. Everyone there now felt even more strongly about fighting against these unfair and cruel crimes.

Officer Kunta came running back with three more officers. He quickly filled them in on what was happening. "We've got the house locked down," he announced. "Every bad guy is handcuffed and sitting in the front yard. And get this—this amazing girl, Aya Diouf, she actually took down Scorpion himself in the basement!"

"Scorpion?" the federal agent cut in, sounding super surprised. "THE Scorpion? We're dealing with HIS gang?"

"You bet," Officer Kunta nodded. "And this kid right here," he pointed at Boubou, "he bravely tackled Greybeard Bounty, one of Scorpion's buddies. Kept him pinned down until we could get there. With the three we just caught, that's the whole gang wrapped up."

"Great job, but we're not done yet," the federal agent said seriously. "Our next target is the big boss—Colonel Parker. He's a tough ex-soldier and really dangerous. He's on a ship offshore. We're going to catch him, and that should shut down their whole operation for good. Got it?"

"Yes, sir!" The officers all shouted together, sounding excited.

Everyone piled into the motorboat, with Boubou jumping in next to Pierre, who was driving. The boat backed into the broader part of the cove before speeding up and heading towards Zinguichou Bay.

"We should be able to see the ship once we're past the bay," the federal agent said, squinting his eyes as he looked at the ocean. "Colonel Parker's probably anchored just off the coast."

Boubou felt excitement and nerves as the boat bounced over the waves. He'd never been part of an actual police operation before, and now he was helping catch one of the most dangerous criminals in Africa!

"Keep your eyes peeled, everyone," the agent said over the engine's sound. "We're looking for a medium-sized cargo ship. It might not have any lights on to avoid being spotted."

As they cleared the bay, the vast expanse of the ocean opened up before them. The moon peeked out from behind some clouds, casting a silvery glow on the water. Boubou and Pierre scanned the horizon, looking for any sign of the ship.

Suddenly, Pierre pointed. "There! I think I see something!"

Everyone turned to look where he was pointing. Sure enough, in the distance, they could make out the dark shape of a ship against the night sky.

"Good eye, kid," the agent said, patting Pierre on the shoulder. "That's got to be it. Okay, team, here's the plan. We're going to approach quietly and cut the engine when we get close. We'll board from both sides—half the team on port, half on starboard. Remember, these guys are dangerous, so stay alert. And you two," he looked at Boubou and Pierre, "you stay in the boat, got it? This is too risky for civilians."

Boubou wanted to argue, to say he could help, but he knew the agent was right. This wasn't a game—it was real and really dangerous.

As they got closer to the ship, Boubou's heart was pounding. He watched as the officers checked their gear one last time. The boat slowed, barely making a sound as it glided towards the looming shape of Colonel Parker's ship.

This was it—the final showdown. Boubou held his breath as the officers prepared to board, hoping that soon, this whole crazy adventure would be over and the bad guys would finally be stopped for good.

CHAPTER TWENTY THREE

Waves Of Courage

Under the cover of night, the Riviera and her crew sliced through the water, a sleek shadow moving with the dark waves. The only light came from a half-moon, casting a silvery glow over the sea, making it look like a shimmering metal sheet. Each crew member moved silently, their senses sharp, alert to every sound and movement.

Perched at the front, Boubou peered into the darkness with intense concentration. The cool night air brushed against his face, carrying the salty smell of the sea. Now used to the dim light, his eyes scanned the horizon tirelessly. The tension was thick; everyone knew that the success of their mission depended on staying undetected.

Suddenly, Boubou's hand shot up, signaling the others. He had spotted it—a faint outline of a boat in the distance, barely visible against the dark night sky. Parker's boat was anchored alone, unaware of the approaching danger.

With a quick nod to Boubou, Pierre adjusted the Riviera's course. They approached very carefully, the motor now barely a whisper against the gentle lapping of the waves. Each crew member was completely focused, their breathing controlled, and their movements careful.

As they drew nearer, the outline of Parker's boat became clearer. It was larger than they had expected, a huge mass of metal and wood that seemed to tower over them. The moonlight played tricks on their eyes, casting deep shadows that could hide any number of threats.

The Riviera's crew readied themselves, their hearts pounding. They were close now, close enough to make out the details of the other boat—the ropes, the deck, the faint outline of a figure patrolling.

Boubou felt a rush of excitement as they edged closer, the gap between the two boats narrowing with each passing second. He knew they were about to enter real danger, and the thought sent him a thrill of fear and excitement.

Pierre cut the engine completely, and for a moment, there was nothing but the sound of the sea and their own quiet breaths. Then, working together, they began to paddle, their oars dipping silently into the water, moving them forward like ghosts.

They were mere shadows on the water, inching closer to their target. Boubou could feel his pulse in his ears, the tension building to an almost unbearable level. They were so close now, close enough to hear the creak of wood from Parker's boat, the soft murmur of voices.

The moment of truth was upon them. The task force officers were ready to board, to face whatever awaited them on that ship. Pierre tightened his grip on the steering, with Boubou standing next to him, their eyes fixed on the target. The night, once their cloak of invisibility, was about to witness their boldest move yet.

The peaceful night exploded into chaos when Colonel Parker's massive boat dropped its anchor without warning. The colossal metal weight crashed through the side of the smaller Riviera, tearing a giant hole in its hull. Water gushed in fast, like a waterfall in reverse.

The Riviera rocked violently, sending two task force officers flying overboard with a splash. Panic spread through the crew like wildfire.

"It's a trick! They knew we were coming!" Sergeant Davis yelled, his voice a mix of disbelief and anger. He stumbled, trying to keep his balance on the tilting deck.

Pierre gripped the steering wheel so hard his knuckles turned white, fighting to control the dying boat. "We've been set up!" he shouted, his eyes wide with fear. "Everyone, watch out!"

Boubou clung to the railing, searching the dark waves. "Over there!" he called out, pointing. "I see him!"

One of the officers leaned dangerously far over the side, reaching for his friend in the water. "Hang on, buddy! I've got you!" he yelled, straining against the pull of the sea.

Suddenly, gunshots rang out from Parker's boat. Bullets zipped through the air like angry hornets, pinging off the Riviera's metal sides and splashing into the water around them.

"Take cover!" Sergeant Davis ordered. Everyone on the Riviera dove into the water, desperate to escape the deadly rain of bullets. They huddled behind their sinking boat or swam out of range, hearts pounding.

Boubou and Pierre surfaced behind the boat, gasping for air. Boubou spit out a mouthful of salty water. "We need a plan, fast!" he panted.

The Sergeant nodded, his mind racing. "We swim to Parker's boat," he said, his voice tense. "Stay low. Find a blind spot."

Pierre joined them, adding, "It's our only chance. We have to surprise them now. Let's move!"

The team started swimming toward Parker's boat, each stroke bringing them closer to danger—their only hope of turning things around. Bullets continued to fly overhead, a terrifying soundtrack to their desperate mission.

As they swam, Boubou's mind raced. He thought about Aya, their village, and everything that had led them to this moment. He pushed through the exhaustion, determined to make it through this night alive.

They finally reached a safe spot after what felt like hours, but it was only seconds. The gunfire stopped, leaving only the sound of their heavy breathing and gentle waves.

"This is it," Sergeant Davis whispered as they neared the enemy boat. "We're safe, for now."

Boubou and Pierre were treading water, watching helplessly as the Riviera sank into the dark ocean. Suddenly, an idea hit Boubou like a bolt of lightning. He turned to Sergeant Davis, his eyes shining with determination. "Do you have a lighter?" he asked urgently.

The Sergeant handed over his lighter without hesitation. Boubou took a deep breath, his heart pounding. This was their last chance. He dove underwater, swimming back to the sinking Riviera with all his strength.

Reaching the doomed boat, Boubou quickly found an old, greasy rag hanging near the gas tank. Moving fast, he opened the tank and stuffed most of the rag inside, leaving a bit hanging out like a fuse. He flicked the lighter with shaking hands and set the rag on fire.

Knowing he had only seconds, Boubou plunged back into the water. He swam harder than he ever had in his life, fighting against his heavy, wet clothes and the drag of the sea.

Breaking the surface, Boubou gasped for air. "Move!" he shouted to the others. "Get as far away as you can!"

The team understood immediately. They swam with renewed energy toward the back of Colonel Parker's boat, glancing back nervously at the Riviera.

The night exploded just as they took a deep breath, and dove underwater. The Riviera erupted in a massive fireball, sending burning debris flying everywhere.

When they surfaced, gasping for air, they saw the damage. A huge, flaming hole had been torn in the side of Parker's boat. The once-mighty ship was already starting to sink, fire spreading through it like an angry red monster. They could hear panicked yelling from below deck.

Boubou locked eyes with Sergeant Davis. "We need to get to their rescue raft at the back of the boat," he said urgently. "Now!"

"Right behind you," the Sergeant replied, already swimming toward the stern.

They found the raft and began cutting through the ropes holding it to the sinking ship. Their fingers were clumsy from the cold water, but desperation gave them strength.

"Hurry!" Pierre called out, watching the flames spread.

Finally, the ropes gave way. Working together, they lowered the raft into the water and climbed aboard, collapsing in exhaustion.

As they rowed away from the burning wreckage, Boubou watched members of Parker's crew jump into the dark water to escape the flames. He felt a mix of emotions—relief, sadness, and a strange kind of pride.

"You did it, kid," Sergeant Davis said, looking at Boubou with newfound respect. "You actually did it."

Boubou stared at the burning remains of the Riviera, feeling a pang of guilt. He turned to Pierre. "I'm really sorry about your dad's boat," he said softly.

Pierre was quiet for a moment, then nodded. "He would've understood," he said, his voice barely audible over the crackling flames and lapping waves. "We did what we had to do."

As they rowed further into the darkness, leaving the fiery glow behind, Boubou thought about everything that had happened. Their mission had succeeded but at a high cost. He knew the memory of this night—the bravery, the sacrifice, the Riviera's last stand—would stay with him forever.

Safe in their rescue raft, Sergeant Davis and his team circled the scattered smugglers bobbing in the water. Each smuggler clung to bits of wreckage, looking completely beaten and exhausted. They gave up without a fight.

"I think we got them all," Officer Kunta said, counting the captured smugglers. He squinted at the horizon, frowning. "But I don't see Colonel Parker anywhere."

Sergeant Davis scanned the scene, his face grim. "Parker must have either burned up in the fire or drowned," he said. "Can't say I'm sorry about that."

One of the team members checked their gear and groaned. "Our radios are fried," he announced. "Too much water damage."

Pierre's eyes lit up. He dug through the raft's storage compartments like a kid searching for buried treasure. "Got it!" he yelled, holding up a bright orange box.

"Perfect," Sergeant Davis grinned. "Let's call for backup."

Pierre pulled out a flare gun and fired it into the night sky. The bright red light zoomed upward, exploding like a firework. It hung there, painting everything in an eerie glow.

Boubou watched, amazed. He'd seen fireworks before, but never like this. The flare seemed to say, "We're here! We made it!"

It didn't take long for help to arrive. A big task force boat chugged toward them, following the flare like a giant firefly. Boubou and the others watched as the boat fished out Colonel Parker's gang one by one.

"Huh," Kunta muttered, scratching his head. "Still no sign of Parker."

Boubou felt a chill run down his spine. What if Parker had somehow escaped? He pushed the thought away. The smuggler leader had probably died in the explosion or drowned in the cold, dark water. Still, not knowing for sure made Boubou uneasy.

"Looks like we turned the tables on them," Boubou said, trying to sound tough. Inside, he felt a mix of relief, pride, and a little bit of fear.

Sergeant Davis nodded, the tension finally leaving his shoulders. "It's over, boys," he sighed. "We did it."

As they watched the criminals being handcuffed and loaded onto the boat, Boubou thought about everything that had happened. It felt like something out of an action movie, but it had been real—dangerously real. He knew he'd never forget this night or the courage it took to make it through.

Pierre nudged him. "Hey," he said softly. "We make a pretty good team, huh?"

Boubou grinned, feeling a warm glow of friendship. "Yeah," he replied. "I guess we do."

The rescue boat pulled up alongside their raft. Boubou took one last look at the dark ocean as they climbed aboard to safety. Somewhere out there were the remains of the Riviera and Colonel Parker's ship. He silently thanked the sea for giving them a chance to be heroes, just for one night.

Once the smugglers were secured, the task force boat turned its attention to the raft. "Let's get you back to shore," one of the rescuers called out as they approached Sergeant Davis and his team.

The ride back was quiet, each member lost in their thoughts, processing the night's wild events. When the shoreline finally came into view, it looked like the most welcome sight in the world—a promise of safety after a night full of danger and uncertainty.

As they arrived at the house, a group welcomed them with steaming cups of hot chocolate. Aya, her face beaming, ran to greet Boubou. "Hey, bro!" she called out, her voice filled with joy and relief.

When he saw his sister, Boubou felt a massive wave of relief. "Aya, you're okay!" he exclaimed, his voice reflecting how worried he'd been about her chasing down Scorpion.

"Yeah, I'm fine, thanks to these guys," Aya replied, her eyes sparkling with gratitude and a hint of her usual boldness. "But you look like you've been through a hurricane!"

"Hurricane and then some. We've had quite the adventure at sea," said Pierre, still dripping seawater.

Sergeant Davis joined the group, clutching his mug of hot chocolate. "An adventure is one way to put it," he added with a wry smile.

The Sergeant looked around at the group and raised his mug slightly in a toast. "I have to congratulate you kids for your courage tonight. Your actions were pretty crazy but incredibly brave. You showed amazing determination out there. Well done." His words were filled with admiration and a touch of awe at the risks they'd taken and the strength they'd shown.

Sergeant Davis continued, his tone more serious, "But next time, leave it to the professionals. Don't take on such dangerous situations on your own. You risked your lives out there. If you ever find yourselves in trouble like this again, go to the police first. We're here to handle these risks, so you don't have to."

With a hint of defiance in her voice, Aya responded, "We did go to the police first, but that didn't exactly work out." As she spoke, her gaze shifted towards the front of the house, drawing everyone's attention to Chief Gaye.

There he was, sitting on the porch steps, chomping on a giant sandwich. He was surrounded by a couple of other officers, dramatically telling an over-the-top version of his capture and supposedly brave escape. They could hear him boasting about how he single-handedly fought off a bunch of armed smugglers and even claimed to have faced Scorpion himself.

The difference between his tall tales and what really happened wasn't lost on anyone in the front yard, causing amusement and disbelief.

"But the Chief is alive, we're all here, and that's what matters," Boubou said diplomatically. He and Aya exchanged knowing looks, their bond stronger than ever after the night's events.

The Sergeant finally allowed himself a small smile. "A good cup of hot chocolate," he mused. "Sometimes, that's all you need after a night like this."

Sipping his drink, Pierre added, "And maybe a new boat."

Pierre's comment was met with a burst of laughter from everyone. This laughter wasn't just releasing stress—it showed how Pierre could still joke around, even after losing his dad's boat. His ability to find humor after everything that happened brought a moment of much-needed lightness to the group.

As they enjoyed their hot chocolate, the first light of dawn began to break over the horizon, casting a warm glow over the tired but victorious team. They had faced danger head-on and come out stronger, united by their shared courage and determination. Now calm and glistening in the early morning light, the sea seemed to echo the promise of new beginnings and the enduring spirit of those who dare to face their fears.

CHAPTER TWENTY FOUR

Unraveling The Enigma

THE DIOUF SIBLINGS BECAME INSTANT CELEBRITIES IN Zinguichou. News of their daring capture of Scorpion and his entire gang spread like wildfire through the town. By sunrise, the local newspaper was plastered with headlines depicting hope for a brighter future.

"Can you believe it?" Aya exclaimed, waving the newspaper. "We're on the front page!"

Boubou grinned, scanning the article. "They're calling us heroes, Aya. Heroes!"

The town buzzed with excitement, everyone talking about how the takedown of these criminals would transform Zinguichou. No more shady sweatshops or dangerous diamond smuggling. People walked with a spring in their step, their smiles wider than ever before.

Meanwhile, Pierre was basking in his newfound fame among the Diouf siblings' friends. He held court in the local ice cream shop, regaling his audience with tales of the heart-pounding boat chase and gunfight with the smugglers.

"There I was," Pierre said, gesturing dramatically, "waves crashing around us, bullets whizzing past my ears. I knew I had to think fast, or we'd all be fish food!"

His friends leaned in, hanging on every word. Even the loss of his dad's boat couldn't dampen Pierre's spirits. His father had surprised everyone with his reaction.

"Son," he'd said, clapping Pierre on the shoulder, "boats can be replaced. You can't. I'm just glad you're safe and sound."

This only made Pierre even cooler in his friends' eyes. Who wouldn't want a dad like that?

The next afternoon, the gang gathered in their usual hangout spot— the Sambou family's converted barn. Once a dusty storage space, they'd transformed it into the ultimate game room, complete with a foosball table, dart board, and comfy beanbag chairs. It was their fortress of fun, the very place where they'd cooked up their scheme to outsmart the police during the infamous Lighthouse diamond heist.

Adama Sambou flopped onto a beanbag, a hint of jealousy in his voice. "Man, Pierre got all the action. We missed out on the excitement of a lifetime!"

Boubou nodded, his eyes gleaming. "That motorboat was a lifesaver. I can't count how many times I wished we were all there, right in the thick of things."

Djilly shuddered, shaking his head. "No way, dude. Being out on the ocean in the pitch black? That's like asking for trouble. I've said it before, and I'll say it again—bad idea central!"

Amath chimed in with a grin. "Maybe if it was in a submarine, I'd consider it. But let's face it, in the water, I'm about as graceful as a penguin on roller skates. I'd probably end up doing the world's slowest backstroke while being chased by a great white!"

The group erupted in laughter, picturing Amath flailing around in the water with a shark fin circling him.

Bacary's eyes lit up with excitement. "Using the boat as a decoy was genius! It's like something straight out of a war movie, you know? Back in the day, they'd use ships packed with explosives as decoys. Sail 'em right up to the enemy, and KABOOM! Sunk those ships without firing a single shot. Just like your little adventure, minus the explosions and plus a whole lot of teenage adrenaline!"

Bouma punched the air, grinning from ear to ear. "Man, I wish I could've been there to throw down with those smugglers. Imagine me dishing out some good old-fashioned knuckle sandwiches!"

Mouhamed smirked, shaking his head. "Trust me, it's better I wasn't there. In a fight? I'd be about as useful as a screen door on a submarine. Picture this: I wind up for a punch, my invisible opponent ducks, and suddenly, I'm the undefeated champion of fighting thin air! Next thing you know, I'm getting a medal for my brave battle against oxygen."

The room filled with laughter as they imagined Mouhamed in an epic showdown with his formidable foe—absolutely nothing.

Aminata leaned forward, her eyes sparkling with curiosity. "So, are you guys really getting the reward for catching Scorpion?"

Boubou's smile faltered a bit. "Well, not all of it. Chief Gaye's taking half. The rest is split between Aya and me."

"That's so not fair!" Adama burst out, his face scrunching up in indignation.

Aya rolled her eyes dramatically. "Oh, you should hear Chief Gaye talk about it. He's convinced the government guys that he was the mastermind behind Scorpion's capture. It's like we were just his sidekicks or something."

Pierre snorted. "I heard him tell the task force men that he single-handedly tracked Scorpion through the jungle for days."

Adama laughed. "The jungle? What jungle? I heard he claimed he defused a 'highly sophisticated' bomb all by himself."

"Yeah, and he also told the press that he had Scorpion cornered and outsmarted him with some elaborate plan," Mouhamed added, shaking his head.

"Meanwhile, he was hiding behind us the whole time," Aya added.

Bacary chimed in, "I read he even said he went undercover and infiltrated Scorpion's gang."

Aya chuckled. "Can you imagine Chief Gaye undercover? He'd stick out like a sore thumb!"

Adama sighed. "The best part is when he boasted about his 'expert interrogation techniques' that got Scorpion to confess everything. I'm pretty sure Scorpion just laughed at him."

Boubou couldn't help but join in. "And the way he described himself as the 'unsung hero' who brought down a dangerous criminal network? Please, he couldn't even figure out how to use a walkie-talkie properly."

Adama grinned. "Yeah, remember when he kept pressing the wrong button and talking to himself?"

Aya laughed. "Classic Chief Gaye. Always the hero in his own stories."

Boubou smiled, shaking his head. "Well, hero or not, we still had to find him. He's our Chief of police, after all. Who knows what kind of trouble he'll get himself into next time."

Aminata patted Boubou's arm sympathetically. "But hey, who needs credit when you've got the satisfaction of saving the town, right? It's not like you guys were in it for the fame and fortune."

Pierre chuckled, trying to lighten the mood. "Look on the bright side—the Chief's little 'vacation' with the smugglers helped him lose a few pounds. It's like an extreme weight loss program, but with more danger and less kale smoothies."

"Oh, don't worry about him," Mouhamed added with a grin. "I bet he'll be back to his old self in no time. His wife's probably force-feeding him cake as we speak." The group burst into giggles, picturing the rotund Chief struggling to escape a mountain of desserts.

Bacary, always the voice of reason, spoke up. "Half the reward is still pretty awesome. You can't complain about that. So, what's going to happen to Scorpion now?"

Boubou's expression turned serious. "He's headed for a maximum-security prison. No more terrorizing Zinguichou for him."

"And don't forget," Aya added, her voice low, "he killed Kambossa, that grumpy old miser."

Aminata gasped, her hand flying to her mouth. "He murdered him? For real?"

Boubou nodded grimly. "Yeah, the government agents uncovered that during their investigation. The task force director from Dakar called Grandma this morning. He wants us to come down to the police station where they're holding Scorpion."

"Whoa," Bacary whispered, his eyes wide. "This is like something out of a crime show."

"There's more," Boubou continued. "The Chief mentioned that our dad was onto something years ago. He always suspected there was a connection between Scorpion's shady business and Kambossa's place. He just never figured out exactly how they were linked."

A hush fell over the group as they absorbed this new information. The adventure might be over, but the mystery was far from solved. As they sat in their cozy hideout, surrounded by the remnants of their childhood, they realized that growing up in Zinguichou turned out to be far more exciting—and dangerous—than they'd ever imagined.

Old Man Kambossa's life changed forever on a stormy summer day. The crusty fisherman was out on his rickety boat, casting nets near the towering cliffs that guarded Zinguichou's coast. Without warning, angry clouds rolled in, and the sea turned wild.

"Aw, barnacles!" Kambossa growled, fighting to control his boat as waves tossed it around like a toy.

CRASH! A massive wave slammed the boat against the cliff face. Kambossa's stomach lurched as he spiraled into a hidden cove. Trapped by the raging storm, he had no choice but to wait it out.

As Kambossa explored the cove, his weathered hands brushing against slick rock walls, he noticed something odd. Almost invisible among the shadows was a cave entrance with ancient stone steps leading up into darkness.

"Well, I'll be a fish's uncle," Kambossa muttered, his curiosity getting the better of him.

Heart pounding, he climbed the stairs. What he found made his jaw drop: the cave was packed with old wooden chests overflowing with gold coins, jewels, and priceless artifacts!

"Holy mackerel!" Kambossa gasped, picking up a handful of gold doubloons. "This is… this is a pirate treasure!"

He was right. Kambossa had stumbled upon a secret stash hidden by smugglers centuries ago, during the golden age of pirates. It was the discovery of a lifetime, and Kambossa knew he had to keep it under wraps.

With dollar signs in his eyes, Kambossa hatched a plan. He built a house right above the cliff, directly above the secret cave. For years, he worked secretly, carving out tunnels and passages in the cliff like a human mole.

His masterpiece? A hidden tunnel stretching from his backyard shed all the way down to the treasure cave. It was the perfect setup— or so he thought.

In Zinguichou, secrets had a way of getting out. People started to notice Kambossa's sudden splurges: a shiny new boat, fancy fishing gear, and even imported spices and fabrics from the city. Tongues began to wag.

"Where's old Kambossa getting all this cash?" folks whispered. "Did he find buried treasure or something?"

Word spread beyond their sleepy town, catching the attention of some evil dudes—the Scorpion gang. These criminals were always on the hunt for easy money, and Kambossa's mysterious fortune was too juicy to ignore.

It didn't take Scorpion and his goons long to sniff out the truth. One night, they cornered Kambossa, threats flying.

"Nice little setup you've got here, old man," Scorpion hissed. "Be a shame if the cops found out, wouldn't it? Unless… you want to make a deal?"

Kambossa, trapped like a fish in a net, had no choice but to agree. Scorpion quickly realized the hidden cove and cave were perfect for his shady business. He could smuggle all sorts of illegal stuff right under everyone's noses.

But Kambossa grew more miserable by the day. He hated working with these crooks and how they used his secret place for their dirty deeds. One night, he couldn't take it anymore.

"I'm done!" Kambossa shouted at Scorpion. "This ends now!"

Their argument turned ugly fast. In a burst of violence that shocked even his hardened crew, Scorpion did the unthinkable—he killed Kambossa.

After that, Scorpion got clever. He made sure Kambossa's house looked abandoned, spreading rumors that it was haunted. Kids in town dared each other to go near the "ghost house," never knowing the real horrors hiding inside.

Everything was going smoothly for Scorpion and his gang. That is, until two curious kids named Boubou and Aya Diouf showed up, about to turn their whole operation upside down.

❖

"So what's the deal with Chief Gaye's kidnapping?" Aminata asked, leaning forward with excitement. "Sounds like there's more to the story!"

Boubou and Aya exchanged mischievous grins before filling in their friends on the Chief's wild adventure.

"After the Lighthouse fiasco, Chief Gaye was determined not to be the town laughingstock again," Boubou explained. "Especially not because of us meddling kids."

Aya picked up the story. "He was actually on his way to check out this suspicious guy named Hounsou at the Touma salt farm. But he decided to swing by Kambossa's house first, just in case we were onto something."

"Big mistake," Boubou said, shaking his head. "The smugglers spotted him snooping around and grabbed him. They even tried to force him to sign a letter saying he was working with Scorpion's gang!"

"No way!" gasped Mouhamed.

"Way," Aya confirmed. "But Chief Gaye refused to sign. He was sure his team would come to rescue him."

"That's when things got really crazy," Boubou continued. "This guy they called Greybeard? He was like an evil genius at forging signatures. He whipped up a fake note with the Chief's handwriting, throwing everyone off the scent for a while."

The gang exchanged wide-eyed looks, still processing the twists and turns of the story.

Bacary raised his hand. "Hold up. What about that Hounsou guy locked in the basement? Didn't you say Scorpion was about to... you know..." He made a slicing motion across his throat.

"Oh yeah, that's the guy we rescued in the bay," Boubou explained. "He told us his name was Hounsou, but that was a lie. His real name is Sato, and get this—he was actually one of the smugglers!"

"Plot twist!" Amath exclaimed.

Pushing his glasses up his nose, Abdou asked, "So why was Scorpion after him that day?"

Boubou leaned in, lowering his voice dramatically. "Sato got greedy. He was mad because he didn't get his full cut from their last job. He threatened to rat out Scorpion to the cops. The gang locked him up, but he managed to escape on a motorboat. That's when they chased him down, trying to either blow him up or drown him."

"But you and Aya saved him, right?" Aminata said, looking at Boubou with admiration.

Aya rolled her eyes. "We got him to shore, yeah. We left him at the Touma farm, but the smugglers snatched him again the next day. That's where I found him in Kambossa's basement."

"Whoa, Aya!" Adama exclaimed. "You went toe-to-toe with Scorpion? Spill!"

Aya's eyes lit up as she recounted her showdown. "Picture this: I'm in this creepy, dark basement. Scorpion's about to finish off Sato. I knew I had to act fast. Without thinking, I grabbed the first thing I could—a bottle. WHAM! I smashed it right on Scorpion's head!"

"No way!" Mouhamed gasped.

"Way," Aya grinned. "He was stunned just long enough for me to grab his club and knock him down. But Scorpion was tough. He kicked me hard, and I stumbled back. That's when I saw his gun, just out of reach. I lunged for it, my heart pounding like crazy. It was like something out of an action movie, only it was real, and I was holding the gun!"

The group sat in stunned silence, completely enthralled by Aya's tale.

Djilly scratched his head. "But what about those creepy yells we heard at the farmhouse that first day?"

"Oh, that was all part of their master plan," Boubou explained. "They had this not-so-bright guy in the gang stationed there to scare people off with all that shrieking. Remember your missing gas, Adama? That was his handiwork, too."

"After we showed up, they got paranoid," Aya added. "They thought we might bring the cops snooping around. So they had Greybeard, his wife, and another guy pretend they were just renting the place."

Mouhamed's face fell. "So… no real ghosts?"

Aya laughed. "Not a single spook. Scorpion spilled everything this morning during his confession. The task force director filled us in on all the details."

Boubou wrapped up the story. "The whole gang's behind bars now, except for Colonel Parker. He… well, he drowned during the final chase. Sato—or 'Hounsou'—was the key to cracking the case. He'd been their prisoner for ages, and when he turned on them, the whole operation came crashing down. He told the cops everything—how long they'd been smuggling, how Scorpion took over Kambossa's house after… you know. The whole nine yards."

"Wow," Bacary whispered. "Sato really sang like a canary, huh?"

"You bet," Boubou nodded. "He revealed so much that Scorpion knew the jig was up. He just gave in and confessed to everything."

Adama groaned dramatically. "Just my luck! I was there for the creepy guy and getting chased off by Greybeard, but I missed all the real action at the end!"

"Trust me, it wasn't exactly a party," Aya said seriously. "Getting caught by smugglers in a cave while trying to rescue the Chief? Not fun."

"And hiding in that attic with bullets flying everywhere was terrifying," Boubou added. "I honestly thought we were goners."

Adama's expression softened. "Yeah, I guess it wasn't all thrills and chills. You guys really earned whatever reward you get."

Aya's face lit up. "Speaking of the reward—we're planning a huge celebration feast for everyone once we get it!"

"Now you're talking!" Adama whooped, doing a spontaneous cartwheel across the room.

The mood in the barn lightened as the friends began excitedly planning their upcoming feast, the dangers of their adventure already fading into an exciting memory.

CHAPTER TWENTY FIVE

New Horizons

THE DIOUF SIBLINGS COULD HARDLY BELIEVE THEIR EYES when they saw the reward money: $50,000! The Zakar task force praised them for catching Scorpion, a criminal they'd been chasing for ages.

"We've got to celebrate!" Aya exclaimed, already planning a party in Adama's barn. Her mind raced with ideas for decorations, food, and games.

But fate had other plans. Countess Mbaye, who'd grown fond of the kids since they recovered her stolen diamonds, called Grandma Diouf with an offer they couldn't refuse.

"Let me host your celebration at the Lighthouse," the Countess insisted. "It'll be a night to remember!"

And boy, was she right! The dinner at the Lighthouse was the talk of the town, making headlines all over Zinguichou. For the kids, this second Lighthouse dinner was even more epic than the first, a perfect end to their wild adventure.

The grand dining room of the Lighthouse was decked out in style. Crystal chandeliers sparkled overhead, casting a warm glow on the elegant table settings. The aroma of delicious food filled the air, making everyone's mouths water.

At the table, Adama dug into his third serving of ice cream, his eyes sparkling with excitement. "Wouldn't it be awesome if we solved a new mystery every week?" he daydreamed, waving his spoon for emphasis. "And celebrated like this each time? Man, that would be the life!"

The others laughed, knowing life wasn't quite that convenient. But they all felt certain more thrilling adventures lay ahead. Their Detective stories had become local legends, with everyone in Zinguichou eagerly waiting to hear what the Diouf siblings would do next.

"I can see it now," Boubou chimed in, grinning. "The Amazing Adventures of the Diouf Detective Agency! We'd be famous all over Africa!"

"Don't forget about us sidekicks," Mouhamed added with a wink. "Every great Detective needs a trusty team, right?"

Pierre savored his last spoonful of ice cream, aware of the envious glances from his friends. "You know," he said, leaning back in his chair, "I used to beg my dad for a car. He got a motorboat instead, and I was so bummed. But now? Best. Decision. Ever. That boat gave me more excitement in one day than I've had since moving to Africa!"

"Who knew a fishing trip could turn into a high-speed chase?" Aya laughed, remembering their wild adventure on the water.

Just then, Countess Mbaye swept into the room, her elegant dress rustling as she walked. Her brother Ibrahima was close behind, looking just as mysterious. With a smile that hinted at secrets, she announced, "Everyone, please join me outside. We have a surprise waiting for you all!"

Curious whispers broke out as the gang pushed back their chairs and followed the Countess. What could possibly top this fantastic dinner? They filed into the cool night air, the stars twinkling overhead like a thousand tiny diamonds.

There, under the moonlight, sat a sight that made their jaws drop—a brand-new motorboat, sleek and shiny, strapped to a trailer. It was bigger and more impressive than anything they'd imagined, looking like something straight out of a James Bond movie.

Pierre's eyes nearly popped out of his head. He blinked rapidly, sure he must be dreaming. "Is… is that for me?" he stammered, looking from the boat to his friends and back again. "Did you do this?" he asked the Countess, his voice barely above a whisper.

The Countess shook her head, still smiling. "Not from me, Pierre. This is all thanks to your bravery. It's bought with Boubou and Aya's reward money."

"Don't worry," Aya added with a laugh, seeing Pierre's stunned expression. "Grandma Diouf approved! We couldn't think of a better way to spend it."

The boat was a thing of beauty. Its polished hull gleamed in the moonlight, smooth as glass. The leather seats looked butter-soft, inviting everyone to hop in for a ride. The dashboard was lit up like a spaceship control panel, with more gadgets and gizmos than they could count. The motor, nestled at the back, looked powerful enough to make waves all the way to America!

"This is insane!" Adama shouted, practically bouncing with excitement. He circled the boat, running his hand along its side. "It's like something out of a movie!"

Boubou put his hand on Pierre's shoulder, his voice serious despite the grin on his face. "It's more than just a cool boat, buddy. It's to say thanks for your courage and for risking your dad's boat to help us. We couldn't have solved the case without you."

The group crowded around, oohing and aahing over every detail. They peeked inside, marveling at the plush interior and high-tech equipment. Pierre ran his hand along the smooth side, his heart pounding with joy and gratitude.

"I can't believe this," he said, his voice thick with emotion. "Thank you all so much. This is like a dream come true!" He turned to Boubou and Aya, pulling them into a tight hug. "You guys are the best friends anyone could ask for."

Unable to contain his excitement any longer, Pierre turned to the whole group, his eyes shining with anticipation. "What do you say we take this beauty out for a spin first thing tomorrow? We could pack a picnic and make a whole day of it!"

The response was immediate and deafening. Whoops and cheers erupted from the group, their faces lighting up like Christmas morning. High-fives were exchanged and grins stretched from ear to ear as they imagined the adventures waiting for them out on the open water.

"The last one to the dock is a rotten egg!" Adama called out, already planning the race in his head.

"I call dibs on being co-captain!" Mouhamed added, puffing out his chest importantly.

As the excitement swirled around them, Boubou and Aya shared a quiet smile. This was what it was all about—not just solving mysteries but bringing joy to their friends and community.

Standing under the starry sky, admiring their incredible new boat, the night felt electric with possibility. It wasn't just a gift—it was a promise of new horizons, new mysteries to solve, and the unbreakable bond of friendship that would carry them through whatever exciting challenges lay ahead.

CHAPTER TWENTY SIX

Ripples Of Suspicion

THE NEXT MORNING DAWNED BRIGHT AND BEAUTIFUL, THE sky a canvas of oranges and pinks as Pierre and the gang gathered at the dock. The air buzzed with excitement, everyone's eyes fixed on the gleaming motorboat that looked more spaceship than watercraft. Its polished surface caught the early light, seeming to glow with its own energy.

"Holy cow, she's gorgeous!" Adama exclaimed, his jaw practically on the ground.

Pierre couldn't stop grinning. "Isn't she, though?"

"Just wait 'til you see her slice through the water," Boubou added, bouncing on his toes.

Aminata sighed dreamily. "It's like something out of a magazine!"

Aya ran her hand along the sleek surface. "I can't believe we're actually going to ride this beauty."

"Better pinch yourself, Aya, because it's happening," Pierre laughed.

One by one, they clambered aboard, their excited chatter and laughter mixing with the gentle lapping of waves against the hull.

"Everyone find a seat and hold on," Pierre instructed, making sure everyone was settled. "This is going to be a ride to remember."

When Pierre fired up the engine, it came to life with a deep, powerful purr that promised speed and adventure. As they pulled away from the dock, everyone felt a surge of anticipation.

❖

Out on the open water, the boat exceeded all expectations. It cut through the waves like a hot knife through butter, smooth as silk but fast as lightning.

"Whoa! This is incredible!" Boubou shouted, his voice filled with excitement.

The wind whipped their hair into wild tangles, and the occasional spray of cool water had them squealing with delight.

"This is the best!" Aminata yelled, her laughter ringing out over the sound of the engine.

"Hang on tight!" Pierre called over his shoulder, a mischievous glint in his eye as he pushed the throttle forward.

The boat responded instantly, leaping across the water even faster. "Feel that power!" Pierre shouted, exhilarated.

Aya, gripping the side, leaned into the wind. "We're flying!"

Adama's face lit up with joy and added, "I've never felt anything like this! It's amazing!"

They sped across the water, the boat effortlessly handling the waves. The sense of freedom and adventure filled their hearts, making this a day they would never forget.

Whoops and hollers filled the air as they zipped along, leaving a trail of white foam in their wake. Boubou and Aminata clung to the bow, laughing so hard they could barely breathe as they braced against the exhilarating speed. The shoreline blurred into a smear of green and brown, the world narrowing down to just this moment of pure, joyful freedom.

For a while, it was nothing but fun in its purest form. The boat danced on the waves, and their spirits soared right along with it. But amid all the excitement, Aya felt a strange uneasiness creeping in. Something felt… off. She couldn't explain it, but a sense of wrongness nagged at the back of her mind. Standing next to Pierre behind the windshield, she scanned their surroundings nervously. Nothing seemed out of place—the sun shone brightly, the water glittered invitingly, and her friends were still lost in the thrill of the ride.

Almost unconsciously, Aya's hand slipped into her pocket, her fingers finding the familiar, comforting shapes of her secret cowrie shells. The moment she touched them, a flood of images and whispered warnings crashed over her. Aya shivered, despite the warm sun on her skin. The certainty hit her like a punch to the gut—they weren't alone out here. The feeling of being watched prickled along her spine, an unseen threat hanging in the air like storm clouds. She looked at her friends, their faces lit up with joy and excitement, and felt a stab of fear. They were in danger, and they had no idea.

Somewhere along the rocky shoreline, hidden in the shadows, danger was indeed lurking. A pair of cold, calculating eyes never left the boat as it sped across the water. Colonel Parker, a man they thought was long gone, watched and waited. A cruel smile played across his lips as he observed the unsuspecting group, already plotting his revenge.

END OF VOLUME 2

About The Author

Walter Simin is a character. He is a multifaceted author and artist, renowned for his work as a director in film and television, his captivating narratives in children's literature and his evocative paintings exhibited worldwide. With a career that has spanned across Africa for over a decade, Walter embodies a vast African soul in both his literary and artistic endeavors. His diverse background, rich with global experiences, deeply influences his storytelling, infusing his works with authenticity and a broad cultural perspective.

As a father of four and a devoted husband and dog owner, Walter's life is a vibrant blend of family, creativity, and exploration. His debut series, "Boubou & Aya," was inspired by his desire to write adventure books for a friend's son who had lost his mother. Through these stories, Walter aims to help children who have lost parents stay connected with them through imagination, adventure, and magic, showing that their loved ones are still there to guide and support them always. This series is a testament to his ability to weave tales that resonate with both the innocence of childhood and the profound depth of African heritage, while also addressing sensitive emotional experiences.

Beyond writing, Walter's artistic talent extends to the canvas, where his passion for vibrant colors and bold textures translates into stunning paintings that have garnered acclaim in art circles around the world. His work, both as an author and an artist, reflects his profound connection to the African continent, its culture, and its people, making him a unique and compelling voice in the realms of both literature and art.

A FAVOR BEFORE YOU GO...

As we close this volume of « The Adventures Of Boubou & Aya » I hope you enjoyed this journey as much as I loved creating it. Your companionship through these pages has been invaluable.

Now, I have a small but significant request. If you found yourself captivated by the mysteries of Boubou and Aya's world, please leave a review. Whether it's a few words or a detailed account of your experience, your thoughts mean the world to authors like myself, and your feedback helps other readers discover and join in on our adventures.

You can leave your thoughts wherever you purchased the book on your favourite review site, or directly on the book page on Amazon.

Thank you for being a part of this journey, and I can't wait to share more adventures with you in the future!

With heartfelt thanks,

Walter Simin

WANT TO GET SOCIAL?

Let's keep in touch! Connect with me here:

www.waltersimin.com

Facebook: waltersiminbooks
Instagram: @waltersimin
Tiktok: @waltersimin

www.ingramcontent.com/pod-product-compliance
Lightning Source LLC
LaVergne TN
LVHW031323190726
843493LV00013B/3024